ABOUT THE AUTHOR

Photograph copyright © Shane Leonard

STEPHEN KING is the author of more than seventy books, all of them worldwide bestsellers.

The novella is a form King has returned to over and over again, and many have been turned into celebrated films, TV series and streamed events including *1922*, *The Body* (*Stand By Me*) and *Rita Hayworth and Shawshank Redemption* which was the basis of *The Shawshank Redemption*, IMDb's top-rated movie of all time.

King is the recipient of the 2020 Audio Publishers Association Lifetime Achievement Award, the 2018 PEN America Literary Service Award, the 2014 National Medal of Arts, and the 2003 National Book Foundation Medal for Distinguished Contribution to American Letters. He lives in Bangor, Maine, with his wife, novelist Tabitha King.

By Stephen King and published by Hodder & Stoughton

NOVELS:

Carrie
'Salem's Lot
The Shining
The Stand
The Dead Zone
Firestarter
Cujo
Cycle of the Werewolf
Christine
Pet Sematary
It
The Eyes of the Dragon
Misery
The Tommyknockers
The Dark Half
Needful Things
Gerald's Game
Dolores Claiborne
Insomnia
Rose Madder
Desperation
Bag of Bones
The Girl Who Loved Tom Gordon
Dreamcatcher
From a Buick 8
Cell
Lisey's Story
Duma Key
Under the Dome
11.22.63
Doctor Sleep
Mr Mercedes
Revival
Finders Keepers
Enf of Watch
Sleeping Beauties (with Owen King)
The Outsider
Elevation
The Institute

The Dark Tower I: The Gunslinger
The Dark Tower II:
The Drawing of the Three
The Dark Tower III: The Waste Lands
The Dark Tower IV: Wizard and Glass
The Dark Tower V: Wolves of the Calla
The Dark Tower VI: Song of Susannah
The Dark Tower VII: The Dark Tower
The Wind through the Keyhole:
A Dark Tower Novel

As Richard Bachman

Thinner
The Running Man
The Bachman Books
The Regulators
Blaze

STORY COLLECTIONS:

Night Shift
Different Seasons
Skeleton Crew
Four Past Midnight
Nightmares and Dreamscapes
Hearts in Atlantis
Everything's Eventual
Just after Sunset
Stephen King Goes to the Movies
Full Dark, No Stars
The Bazaar of Bad Dreams
If It Bleeds

NON-FICTION:

Danse Macabre
On Writing (A Memoir of the Craft)

1922

'Dripping with American Gothic . . . Utterly convincing and packed with grim atmosphere, it is a story that manages to keep you compulsively turning the pages' – *Independent*

'It's compulsive reading, sometimes scary, revolting, ultimately heartbreaking . . . There is a hint of the supernatural in it, although the borderline between a haunting and madness here is a hairline fracture, and one that King exploits elegantly all the way to the end' – Neil Gaiman, *Guardian*

'Wonderfully gruesome . . . The pages practically turn themselves' – *USA Today*

PRAISE FOR STEPHEN KING

'One of the great storytellers of our time' – *Guardian*

'King readers know that he is an absolute master of the long story' ¬ *Daily Express*

'The true narrative artist is a rare creature. Storytelling – the ability to make the listener or the reader need to know, demand to know, what happens next – is a gift . . . Stephen King, like Charles Dickens before him, has this gift in spades' – *The Times*

STEPHEN KING

1922

HIGH LIFE HIGHLAND	
3800 21 0008531 7	
Askews & Holts	27-Oct-2021
AF	£7.99

Previously published in Great Britain in 2010
in *Full Dark, No Stars* by Hodder & Stoughton
An Hachette UK company

First Hodder paperback edition published 2021

A Hodder Paperback

1

A CIP catalogue record for this title is available from the British Library

B format ISBN 978 1 529 37935 8
eBook ISBN 978 1 529 37936 5

Typeset in Bembo
Printed and bound in Great Britain by Clays Ltd, Elcograf S.p.A.

Hodder & Stoughton policy is to use papers that are natural,
renewable and recyclable products and made from wood grown in sustainable
forests. The logging and manufacturing processes are expected to conform
to the environmental regulations of the country of origin.

Hodder & Stoughton Ltd
Carmelite House
50 Victoria Embankment
London EC4Y 0DZ

www.hodder.co.uk

Publisher's Note: *1922* is also available in the collection *Full Dark, No Stars*,
published by Hodder & Stoughton

1922

Magnolia Hotel
Omaha, Nebraska

TO WHOM IT MAY CONCERN:

My name is Wilfred Leland James, and this is my confession. In June of 1922 I murdered my wife, Arlette Christina Winters James, and hid her body by tupping it down an old well. My son, Henry Freeman James, aided me in this crime, although at 14 he was not responsible; I cozened him into it, playing upon his fears and beating down his quite normal objections over a period of 2 months. This is a thing I regret even more bitterly than the crime, for reasons this document will show.

The issue that led to my crime and damnation was 100 acres of good land in Hemingford Home, Nebraska. It was willed to my wife by John Henry Winters, her father. I wished to add this land to our freehold farm, which in 1922 totaled 80 acres. My wife, who never took to the farming life (or to being a farmer's wife), wished to sell it to the Farrington Company for cash money. When I asked her if she truly wanted to live downwind from a Farrington's hog-butchery, she told me we could sell up the farm as well as her father's acreage – my father's farm, and his before him! When I asked her what we might do with money and no land, she said we could move to Omaha, or even St Louis, and open a shop.

'I will never live in Omaha,' I said. 'Cities are for fools.'

This is ironic, considering where I now live, but I will not live here for long; I know that as well as I know what is making the sounds I hear in the walls. And I know where I shall find myself after this earthly life is done. I wonder if Hell can be worse than the City of Omaha. Perhaps it *is* the City of Omaha, but with no good country surrounding it; only a smoking, brimstone-stinking emptiness full of lost souls like myself.

We argued bitterly over that 100 acres during the winter and spring of 1922. Henry was caught in the middle, yet tended more to my side; he favored his mother in looks but me in his love for the land. He was a biddable lad with none of his mother's arrogance. Again and again he told her that he had no desire to live in Omaha or any city, and would go only if she and I came to an agreement, which we never could.

I thought of going to Law, feeling sure that, as the Husband in the matter, any court in the land would uphold my right to decide the use and purpose of that land. Yet something held me back. 'Twas not fear of the neighbors' chatter, I had no care for country gossip; 'twas something else. I had come to hate her, you see. I had come to wish her dead, and that was what held me back.

I believe that there is another man inside of every man, a stranger, a Conniving Man. And I believe that by March of 1922, when the Hemingford County skies were white and every field was a snow-scrimmed mudsuck, the Conniving Man inside Farmer Wilfred James had already passed judgment on my wife and decided her fate. 'Twas justice of the black-cap variety, too. The Bible says that an ungrateful child is like a serpent's tooth, but a nagging and ungrateful Wife is ever so much sharper than that.

I am not a monster; I tried to save her from the Conniving Man.. I told her that if we could not agree, she should go to her mother's in Lincoln, which is sixty miles west – a good distance for a separation which is not quite a divorce yet signifies a dissolving of the marital corporation.

'And leave you my father's land, I suppose?' she asked,

and tossed her head. How I had come to hate that pert head-toss, so like that of an ill-trained pony, and the little sniff which always accompanied it. 'That will never happen, Wilf.'

I told her that I would buy the land from her, if she insisted. It would have to be over a period of time – eight years, perhaps ten – but I would pay her every cent.

'A little money coming in is worse than none,' she replied (with another sniff and head-toss). 'This is something every woman knows. The Farrington Company will pay all at once, and their idea of top dollar is apt to be far more generous than yours. And I will never live in Lincoln. 'Tis not a city but only a village with more churches than houses.'

Do you see my situation? Do you not understand the 'spot' she put me in? Can I not count on at least a little of your sympathy? No? Then hear this.

In early April of that year – eight years to this very day, for all I know – she came to me all bright and shining. She had spent most of the day at the 'beauty salon' in McCook, and her hair hung around her cheeks in fat curls that reminded me of the toilet-rolls one finds in hotels and inns. She said she'd had an idea. It was that we should sell the 100 acres *and* the farm to the Farrington combine. She believed they would buy it all just to get her father's piece, which was near the railway line (and she was probably right).

'Then,' said this saucy vixen, 'we can split the money, divorce, and start new lives apart from each other. We both know that's what you want.' As if she didn't.

'Ah,' I said (as if giving the idea serious consideration). 'And with which of us does the boy go?'

'Me, of course,' she said, wide-eyed. 'A boy of 14 needs to be with his mother.'

I began to 'work on' Henry that very day, telling

him his mother's latest plan. We were sitting in the hay-mow. I wore my saddest face and spoke in my saddest voice, painting a picture of what his life would be like if his mother was allowed to carry through with this plan: how he would have neither farm nor father, how he would find himself in a much bigger school, all his friends (most since babyhood) left behind, how, once in that new school, he would have to fight for a place among strangers who would laugh at him and call him a country bumpkin. On the other hand, I said, if we could hold onto all the acreage, I was convinced we could pay off our note at the bank by 1925 and live happily debt-free, breathing sweet air instead of watching pig-guts float down our previously clear stream from sun-up to sundown. 'Now what is it you want?' I asked after drawing this picture in as much detail as I could manage.

'To stay here with you, Poppa,' he said. Tears were streaming down his cheeks. 'Why does she have to be such a . . . such a . . .'

'Go on,' I said. 'The truth is never cussing, Son.'

'Such a *bitch*!'

'Because most women are,' I said. 'It's an ineradicable part of their natures. The question is what we're going to do about it.'

But the Conniving Man inside had already thought of the old well behind the cow barn, the one we only used for slop-water because it was so shallow and murky – only 20 feet deep and little more than a sluice. It was just a question of bringing him to it. And I *had* to, surely you see that; I could kill my wife but must save my lovely son. To what purpose the ownership of 180 acres – or a thousand – if you have no one to share them with and pass them on to?

I pretended to be considering Arlette's mad plan to see good cornland turned into a hog-butchery. I asked her to give me time to get used to the idea. She assented. And during the next 2 months I worked on Henry, getting *him* used to a very different idea. 'Twasn't as hard as it might have been; he had his mother's looks (a woman's looks are the honey, you know, that lure men on to the stinging hive) but not her God-awful stubbornness. It was only necessary to paint a picture of what his life would be like in Omaha or St Louis. I raised the possibility that even those two overcrowded antheaps might not satisfy her; she might decide only Chicago would do. 'Then,' I said, 'you might find yourself going to high school with black niggers.'

He grew cold toward his mother; after a few efforts – all clumsy, all rebuffed – to regain his affections, she returned the chill. I (or rather the Conniving Man) rejoiced at this. In early June I told her that, after great consideration, I had decided I would never allow her to sell those 100 acres without a fight; that I would send us all to beggary and ruin if that was what it took.

She was calm. She decided to take legal advice of her own (for the Law, as we know, will befriend whomever pays it). This I foresaw. And smiled at it! Because she couldn't pay for such advice. By then I was holding tight to what little cash money we had. Henry even turned his pig-bank over to me when I asked, so she couldn't steal from that source, paltry as it was. She went, of course, to the Farrington Company offices in Deland, feeling quite sure (as was I) that they who had so much to gain would stand good her legal fees.

'They will, and she'll win,' I told Henry from what had become our usual place of conversation in the hay-mow. I was not entirely sure of this, but I had already taken my decision, which I will not go so far as to call 'a plan.'

'But Poppa, that's not fair!' he cried. Sitting there in the hay, he looked very young, more like 10 than 14.

'Life never is,' I said. 'Sometimes the only thing to do is to take the thing that you must have. Even if someone gets hurt.' I paused, gauging his face. 'Even if someone dies.'

He went white. 'Poppa!'

'If she was gone,' I said, 'everything would be the way it was. All the arguments would cease. We could live here peacefully. I've offered her everything I can to make her go, and she won't. There's only one other thing I can do. That *we* can do.'

'But I love her!'

'I love her, too,' I said. Which, however little you might believe it, was true. The hate I felt toward her in that year of 1922 was greater than a man can feel for any woman unless love is a part of it. And, bitter and willful though she was, Arlette was a warm-natured woman. Our 'marital relations' had never ceased, although since the arguments about the 100 acres had begun, our grapplings in the dark had become more and more like animals rutting.

'It needn't be painful,' I said. 'And when it's over . . . well . . .'

I took him out back of the barn and showed him the well, where he burst into bitter tears. 'No, Poppa. Not that. No matter what.'

But when she came back from Deland (Harlan Cotterie, our nearest neighbor, carried her most of the way in his Ford, leaving her to walk the last two miles) and Henry begged her to 'leave off so we can just be a family again,' she lost her temper, struck him across the mouth, and told him to stop begging like a dog.

'Your father's infected you with his timidity. Worse, he's infected you with his greed.'

As though she were innocent of *that* sin!

'The lawyer assures me the land is mine to do with as I wish, and I'm going to sell it. As for the two of you, you can sit here and smell roasting hogs together and cook your own meals and make your own beds. You, my son, can plow all the day and read *his* everlasting books all night. They've done him little good, but you may get on better. Who knows?'

'Mama, that's not fair!'

She looked at her son as a woman might look at a strange man who had presumed to touch her arm. And how my heart rejoiced when I saw him looking back just as coldly. 'You can go to the devil, both of you. As for me, I'm going to Omaha and opening a dress shop. That's *my* idea of fair.'

This conversation took place in the dusty dooryard between the house and the barn, and her idea of fair was the last word. She marched across the yard, raising dust with her dainty town shoes, went into the house, and slammed the door. Henry turned to look at me. There was blood at the corner of his mouth and his lower lip was swelling. The rage in his eyes was of the raw, pure sort that only adolescents can feel. It is rage that doesn't count the cost. He nodded his head. I nodded back, just as gravely, but inside the Conniving Man was grinning.

That slap was her death-warrant.

Two days later, when Henry came to me in the new corn, I saw he had weakened again. I wasn't dismayed or surprised; the years between childhood and adulthood are gusty years, and those living through them spin like the weathercocks some farmers in the Midwest used to put atop their grain silos.

'We can't,' he said. 'Poppa, she's in Error. And Shannon says those who die in Error go to Hell.'

God damn the Methodist church and Methodist Youth Fellowship, I thought . . . but the Conniving Man only smiled. For the next ten minutes we talked theology in the green corn while early summer clouds — the best clouds, the ones that float like schooners – sailed slowly above us, trailing their shadows like wakes. I explained to him that, quite the opposite of sending Arlette to Hell, we would be sending her to Heaven. 'For,' I said, 'a murdered man or woman dies not in God's time but in Man's. He . . . or she . . . is cut short before he . . . or she . . . can atone for sin, and so all errors must be forgiven. When you think of it that way, every murderer is a Gate of Heaven.'

'But what about us, Poppa? Wouldn't we go to Hell?'

I gestured to the fields, brave with new growth. 'How can you say so, when you see Heaven all around us? Yet she means to drive us away from it as surely as the angel with the flaming sword drove Adam and Eve from the Garden.'

He gazed at me, troubled. Dark. I hated to darken my son in such a way, yet part of me believed then and believes still that it was not I who did it to him, but she.

'And think,' I said. 'If she goes to Omaha, she'll dig herself an even deeper pit in Sheol. If she takes you, you'll become a city boy—'

'I never will!' He cried this so loudly that crows took wing from the fenceline and swirled away into the blue sky like charred paper.

'You're young and you will,' I said. 'You'll forget all this . . . you'll learn city ways . . . and begin digging your own pit.'

If he had returned by saying that murderers had no hope of joining their victims in Heaven, I might have been stumped. But either his theology did not stretch so far or he didn't want to consider such things. And is there Hell, or do we make our own on earth? When I consider the last eight years of my life, I plump for the latter.

'How?' he asked. 'When?'

I told him.

'And we can go on living here after?'

I said we could.

'And it won't hurt her?'

'No,' I said. 'It will be quick.'

He seemed satisfied. And still it might not have happened, if not for Arlette herself.

We settled on a Saturday night about halfway through a June that was as fine as any I can remember. Arlette sometimes took a glass of wine on Summer evenings, although rarely more. There was good reason for this. She was one of those people who can never take two glasses without taking four, then six, then the whole bottle. And another bottle, if there is another. 'I have to be very careful, Wilf. I like it too much. Luckily for me, my willpower is strong.'

That night we sat on the porch, watching the late light linger over the fields, listening to the somnolent *reeeeee* of the crickets. Henry was in his room. He had hardly touched his supper, and as Arlette and I sat on the porch in our matching rockers with the MA and PA seat-cushions, I thought I heard a faint sound that could have been retching. I remember thinking that when the moment came, he would not be able to go through with it. His mother would wake up bad-tempered the following morning with a 'hangover' and no knowledge of how close she had come to never seeing another Nebraska dawn. Yet I moved forward with the plan. Because I was like one of those Russian nesting dolls? Perhaps. Perhaps every man is like that. Inside me was the Conniving Man, but inside the Conniving Man was a Hopeful Man. That fellow died sometime between 1922 and 1930. The Conniving Man, having done his damage, disappeared. Without his schemes and ambitions, life has been a hollow place.

I brought the bottle out to the porch with me, but when I tried to fill her empty glass, she covered it with her hand. 'You needn't get me drunk to get what you want. I want it, too. I've got an itch.' She spread her legs and put her hand on her crotch to show where the itch was. There was a Vulgar Woman inside her – perhaps even a Harlot – and the wine always let her loose.

'Have another glass anyway,' I said. 'We've something to celebrate.'

She looked at me warily. Even a single glass of wine made her eyes wet (as if part of her was weeping for all the wine it wanted and could not have), and in the sunset light they looked orange, like the eyes of a jack-o'-lantern with a candle inside it.

'There will be no suit,' I told her, 'and there will be no divorce. If the Farrington Company can afford to pay us for my 80 as well as your father's 100, our argument is over.'

For the first and only time in our troubled marriage, she actually *gaped*. 'What are you saying? Is it what I think you're saying? Don't fool with me, Wilf!'

'I'm not,' said the Conniving Man. He spoke with hearty sincerity. 'Henry and I have had many conversations about this—'

'You've been thick as thieves, that's true,' she said. She had taken her hand from the top of her glass and I took the opportunity to fill it. 'Always in the hay-mow or sitting on the woodpile or with your heads together in the back field. I thought it was about Shannon Cotterie.' A sniff and a head-toss. But I thought she looked a little wistful, as well. She sipped at her second glass of wine. Two sips of a second glass and she could still put the glass down and go to bed. Four and I might as well hand her the bottle. Not to mention the other two I had standing by.

'No,' I said. 'We haven't been talking about Shannon.' Although I *had* seen Henry holding her hand on occasion as they walked the 2 miles to the Hemingford Home schoolhouse. 'We've been talking about Omaha. He wants to go, I guess.' It wouldn't do to lay it on too thick, not after a single glass of wine and two sips of another. She was suspicious by nature, was my Arlette, always looking for a deeper motive. And of course in this case I had one. 'At least to try it on for size. And Omaha's not that far from Hemingford . . .'

'No. It isn't. As I've told you both a thousand times.' She sipped her wine, and instead of putting the glass down as she had before, she held it. The orange light above the western horizon was deepening to an otherworldly green-purple that seemed to burn in the glass.

'If it were St Louis, that would be a different thing.'

'I've given that idea up,' she said. Which meant, of course, that she had investigated the possibility and found it problematic. Behind my back, of course. All of it behind my back except for the company lawyer. And she would have done *that* behind my back as well, if she hadn't wanted to use it as a club to beat me with.

'Will they buy the whole piece, do you think?' I asked. 'All 180 acres?'

'How would I know?' Sipping. The second glass half-empty. If I told her now that she'd had enough and tried to take it away from her, she'd refuse to give it up.

'You do, I have no doubt,' I said. 'That 180 acres is like St Louis. You've *investigated*.'

She gave me a shrewd sidelong look . . . then burst into harsh laughter. 'P'raps I have.'

'I suppose we could hunt for a house on the outskirts of town,' I said. 'Where there's at least a field or two to look at.'

'Where you'd sit on your ass in a porch-rocker all day, letting your wife do the work for a change? Here, fill this up. If we're celebrating, let's celebrate.'

I filled both. It only took a splash in mine, as I'd taken but a single swallow.

'I thought I might look for work as a mechanic. Cars and trucks, but mostly farm machinery. If I can keep that old Farmall running' – I gestured with my glass toward the dark hulk of the tractor standing beside the barn – 'then I guess I can keep anything running.'

'And Henry talked you into this.'

'He convinced me it would be better to take a chance at being happy in town than to stay here on my own in what would be sure misery.'

'The boy shows sense and the man listens! At long last! Hallelujah!' She drained her glass and held it out for more. She grasped my arm and leaned close enough for me to smell sour grapes on her breath. 'You may get that thing you like tonight, Wilf.' She touched her purple-stained tongue to the middle of her upper lip. 'That *nasty* thing.'

'I'll look forward to that,' I said. If I had my way, an even nastier thing was going to happen that night in the bed we had shared for 15 years.

'Let's have Henry down,' she said. She had begun to slur her words. 'I want to congratulate him on finally seeing the light.' (Have I mentioned that the verb *to thank* was not in my wife's vocabulary? Perhaps not. Perhaps by now I don't need to.) Her eyes lit up as a thought occurred to her. 'We'll give 'im a glass of wine! He's old enough!' She elbowed me like one of the old men you see sitting on the benches that flank the courthouse steps, telling each other dirty jokes. 'If we loosen his tongue a little, we may even find out if he's made any time with Shannon Cotterie . . . . li'l baggage, but she's got pretty hair, I'll give 'er that.'

'Have another glass of wine first,' said the Conniving Man.

She had another two, and that emptied the bottle. (The first one.) By then she was singing 'Avalon' in her best minstrel voice, and doing her best minstrel eye-rolls. It was painful to see and even more painful to hear.

I went into the kitchen to get another bottle of wine, and judged the time was right to call Henry. Although, as I've said, I was not in great hopes. I could only do it if he were my willing accomplice, and in my heart I believed that he would shy from the deed when the talk ran out and the time actually came. If so, we would simply put her to bed. In the morning I would tell her I'd changed my mind about selling my father's land.

Henry came, and nothing in his white, woeful face offered any encouragement for success. 'Poppa, I don't think I can,' he whispered. 'It's *Mama*.'

'If you can't, you can't,' I said, and there was nothing of the Conniving Man in that. I was resigned; what would be would be. 'In any case, she's happy for the first time in months. Drunk, but happy.'

'Not just squiffy? She's *drunk*?'

'Don't be surprised; getting her own way is the only thing that ever makes her happy. Surely 14 years with her is long enough to have taught you that.'

Frowning, he cocked an ear to the porch as the woman who'd given him birth launched into a jarring but word-for-word rendition of 'Dirty McGee.' Henry frowned at this barrelhouse ballad, perhaps because of the chorus ('She was willin' to help him stick it in / For it was Dirty McGee again'), more likely at the way she was slurring the words. Henry had taken the Pledge at a Methodist Youth Fellowship Camp-Out on Labor Day weekend of the year before. I rather enjoyed his shock. When teenagers aren't turning like weathervanes in a high wind, they're as stiff as Puritans.

'She wants you to join us and have a glass of wine.'

'Poppa, you know I promised the Lord I would never drink.'

'You'll have to take that up with her. She wants to have a celebration. We're selling up and moving to Omaha.'

'*No!*'

'Well . . . we'll see. It's really up to you, Son. Come out on the porch.'

His mother rose tipsily to her feet when she saw him, wrapped her arms around his waist, pressed her body rather too tightly against his, and covered his face with extravagant kisses. Unpleasantly smelly ones, from the way he grimaced. The Conniving Man, meanwhile, filled up her glass, which was empty again.

'Finally we're all together! My men see sense!' She raised her glass in a toast, and slopped a goodly portion of it onto her bosom. She laughed and gave me a wink. 'If you're good, Wilf, you can suck it out of the cloth later on.'

Henry looked at her with confused distaste as she plopped back down in her rocker, raised her skirts, and tucked them between her legs. She saw the look and laughed.

'No need to be so prissy. I've seen you with Shannon Cotterie. Li'l baggage, but she's got pretty hair and a nice little figger.' She drank off the rest of her wine and belched. 'If you're not getting a touch of that, you're a fool. Only you'd better be careful. Fourteen's not too young to marry. Out here in the middle, fourteen's not too young to marry your *cousin*.' She laughed some more and held out her glass. I filled it from the second bottle.

'Poppa, she's had enough,' Henry said, as disapproving as a parson. Above us, the first stars were winking into view above that vast flat emptiness I have loved all my life.

'Oh, I don't know,' I said. '*In vino veritas*, that's what Pliny the Elder said . . . in one of those *books* your mother's always sneering about.'

'Hand on the plow all day, nose in a book all night,' Arlette said. 'Except when he's got something else in *me*.'

'*Mama!*'

'*Mama!*' she mocked, then raised her glass in the direction of Harlan Cotterie's farm, although it was too far for us to see the lights. We couldn't have seen them even if it had been a mile closer, now that the corn was high. When summer comes to Nebraska, each farmhouse is a ship sailing a vast green ocean. 'Here's to Shannon Cotterie and her brand-new bubbies, and if my son don't know the color of her nipples, he's a slowpoke.'

My son made no reply to this, but what I could see of his shadowed face made the Conniving Man rejoice.

She turned to Henry, grasped his arm, and spilled wine on his wrist. Ignoring his little mew of distaste, looking into his face with sudden grimness, she said: 'Just make sure that when you're lying down with her in the corn or behind the barn, you're a *no*-poke.' She made her free hand into a fist, poked out the middle finger, then used it to tap a circle around her crotch: left thigh, right thigh, right belly, navel, left belly, back again to the left thigh. 'Explore all you like, and rub around it with your Johnny Mac until he feels good and spits up, but stay out of the home place lest you find yourself locked in for life, just like your mummer and daddy.'

He got up and left, still without a word, and I don't blame him. Even for Arlette, this was a performance of extreme vulgarity. He must have seen her change before his eyes from his mother – a difficult woman but sometimes loving – to a smelly whorehouse madam instructing a green young customer. All bad enough, but he was sweet on the Cotterie girl, and that made it worse. Very young men cannot help but put their first loves on pedestals, and should someone come along and spit on the paragon . . . even if it happens to be one's mother . . .

Faintly, I heard his door slam. And faint but audible sobbing.

'You've hurt his feelings,' I said.

She expressed the opinion that *feelings*, like *fairness*, were also the last resort of weaklings. Then she held out her glass. I filled it, knowing she would remember none of what she'd said in the morning (always supposing she was still there to greet the morning), and would deny it – vehemently – if I told her. I had seen her in this state of drunkenness before, but not for years.

We finished the second bottle (*she* did) and half of the third before her chin dropped onto her wine-stained bosom and she began to snore. Coming through her thus constricted throat, those snores sounded like the growling of an ill-tempered dog.

I put my arm around her shoulders, hooked my hand into her armpit, and hauled her to her feet. She muttered protests and slapped weakly at me with one stinking hand. 'Lea' me 'lone. Want to go to slee'.'

'And you will,' I said. 'But in your bed, not out here on the porch.'

I led her – stumbling and snoring, one eye shut and the other open in a bleary glare – across the sitting room. Henry's door opened. He stood in it, his face expressionless and much older than his years. He nodded at me. Just one single dip of the head, but it told me all I needed to know.

I got her on the bed, took off her shoes, and left her there to snore with her legs spread and one hand dangling off the mattress. I went back into the sitting room and found Henry standing beside the radio Arlette had hounded me into buying the year before.

'She can't say those things about Shannon,' he whispered.

'But she will,' I said. 'It's how she is, how the Lord made her.'

'And she can't take me *away* from Shannon.'

'She'll do that, too,' I said. 'If we let her.'

'Couldn't you . . . Poppa, couldn't you get your own lawyer?'

'Do you think any lawyer whose services I could buy with the little bit of money I have in the bank could stand up to the lawyers Farrington would throw at us? They swing weight in Hemingford County; I swing nothing but a sickle when I want to cut hay. They want that 100 acres and she means for them to have it. This is the only way, but you have to help me. Will you?'

For a long time he said nothing. He lowered his head, and I could see tears dropping from his eyes to the hooked rug. Then he whispered, 'Yes. But if I have to watch it . . . I'm not sure I can . . .'

'There's a way you can help and still not have to watch. Go into the shed and fetch a burlap sack.'

He did as I asked. I went into the kitchen and got her sharpest butcher knife. When he came back with the sack and saw it, his face paled. 'Does it have to be *that*? Can't you . . . with a pillow . . .'

'It would be too slow and too painful,' I said. 'She'd struggle.' He accepted that as if I had killed a dozen women before my wife and thus knew. But I didn't. All I knew was that in all my half-plans – my daydreams of being rid of her, in other words – I had always seen the knife I now held in my hand. And so the knife it would be. The knife or nothing.

We stood there in the glow of the kerosene lamps – there'd be no electricity except for generators in Hemingford Home until 1928 – looking at each other, the great night-silence that exists out there in the middle of things broken only by the unlovely sound of her snores. Yet there was a third presence in that room: her ineluctable will, which existed separate of the woman herself (I thought I sensed it then; these 8 years later I am sure). This is a ghost story, but the ghost was there even before the woman it belonged to died.

'All right, Poppa. We'll . . . we'll send her to Heaven.' Henry's face brightened at the thought. How hideous that seems to me now, especially when I think of how he finished up.

'It will be quick,' I said. Man and boy I've slit nine-score hogs' throats, and I thought it would be. But I was wrong.

Let it be told quickly. On the nights when I can't sleep – and there are many – it plays over and over again, every thrash and cough and drop of blood in exquisite slowness, so let it be told quickly.

We went into the bedroom, me in the lead with the butcher knife in my hand, my son with the burlap sack. We went on tiptoe, but we could have come in clashing cymbals without waking her up. I motioned Henry to stand to my right, by her head. Now we could hear the Big Ben alarm clock ticking on her nightstand as well as her snores, and a curious thought came to me: we were like physicians attending the deathbed of an important patient. But I think physicians at deathbeds do not as a rule tremble with guilt and fear.

Please let there not be too much blood, I thought. *Let the bag catch it. Even better, let him cry off now, at the last minute.*

But he didn't. Perhaps he thought I'd hate him if he did; perhaps he had resigned her to Heaven; perhaps he was remembering that obscene middle finger, poking a circle around her crotch. I don't know. I only know he whispered, 'Goodbye, Mama,' and drew the bag down over her head.

She snorted and tried to twist away. I had meant to reach under the bag to do my business, but he had to push down tightly on it to hold her, and I couldn't. I saw her nose making a shape like a shark's fin in the burlap. I saw the look of panic dawning on his face, too, and knew he wouldn't hold on for long.

I put one knee on the bed and one hand on her shoulder. Then I slashed through the burlap and the throat beneath. She screamed and began to thrash in earnest. Blood welled through the slit in the burlap. Her hands came up and beat the air. Henry stumbled away from the bed with a screech. I tried to hold her. She pulled at the gushing bag with her hands and I slashed at them, cutting three of her fingers to the bone. She shrieked again – a sound as thin and sharp as a sliver of ice – and the hand fell away to twitch on the counterpane. I slashed another bleeding slit in the burlap, and another, and another. Five cuts in all I made before she pushed me away with her unwounded hand and then tore the burlap sack up from her face. She couldn't get it all the way off her head – it caught in her hair – and so she wore it like a snood.

I had cut her throat with the first two slashes, the first time deep enough to show the gristle of her windpipe. With the last two I had carved her cheek and her mouth, the latter so deeply that she wore a clown's grin. It stretched all the way to her ears and showed her teeth. She let loose a guttural, choked roar, the sound a lion might make at feeding-time. Blood flew from her throat all the way to the foot of the counterpane. I remember thinking it looked like the wine when she held her glass up to the last of the daylight.

She tried to get out of bed. I was first dumbfounded, then infuriated. She had been a trouble to me all the days of our marriage and was a trouble even now, at our bloody divorce. But what else should I have expected?

'*Oh Poppa, make her stop!*' Henry shrieked. '*Make her stop, oh Poppa, for the love of God make her stop!*'

I leaped on her like an ardent lover and drove her back down on her blood-drenched pillow. More harsh growls came from deep in her mangled throat. Her eyes rolled in their sockets, gushing tears. I wound my hand into her hair, yanked her head back, and cut her throat yet again. Then I tore the counterpane free from my side of the bed and wrapped it over her head, catching all but the first pulse from her jugular. My face had caught that spray, and hot blood now dripped from my chin, nose, and eyebrows.

Behind me, Henry's shrieks ceased. I turned around and saw that God had taken pity on him (assuming He had not turned His face away when He saw what we were about): he had fainted. Her thrashings began to weaken. At last she lay still . . . but I remained on top of her, pressing down with the counterpane, now soaked with her blood. I reminded myself that she had never done anything easily. And I was right. After thirty seconds (the tinny mail-order clock counted them off), she gave another heave, this time bowing her back so strenuously that she almost threw me off. *Ride 'em, Cowboy*, I thought. Or perhaps I said it aloud. That I can't remember, God help me. Everything else, but not that.

She subsided. I counted another thirty tinny ticks, then thirty after that, for good measure. On the floor, Henry stirred and groaned. He began to sit up, then thought better of it. He crawled into the farthest corner of the room and curled in a ball.

'Henry?' I said.

Nothing from the curled shape in the corner.

'Henry, she's dead. She's dead and I need help.'

Nothing still.

'Henry, it's too late to turn back now. The deed is done. If you don't want to go to prison – and your father to the electric chair – then get on your feet and help me.'

He staggered toward the bed. His hair had fallen into

his eyes; they glittered through the sweat-clumped locks like the eyes of an animal hiding in the bushes. He licked his lips repeatedly.

'Don't step in the blood. We've got more of a mess to clean up in here than I wanted, but we can take care of it. If we don't track it all through the house, that is.'

'Do I have to look at her? Poppa, do I have to *look*?'

'No. Neither of us do.'

We rolled her up, making the counterpane her shroud. Once it was done, I realized we couldn't carry her through the house that way; in my half-plans and daydreams, I had seen no more than a discreet thread of blood marring the counterpane where her cut throat (her *neatly* cut throat) lay beneath. I had not foreseen or even considered the reality: the white counterpane was a blackish-purple in the dim room, oozing blood as a bloated sponge will ooze water.

There was a quilt in the closet. I could not suppress a brief thought of what my mother would think if she could see what use I was making of that lovingly stitched wedding present. I laid it on the floor. We dropped Arlette onto it. Then we rolled her up.

'Quick,' I said. 'Before this starts to drip, too. No . . . wait . . . go for a lamp.'

He was gone so long that I began to fear he'd run away. Then I saw the light come bobbing down the short hall past his bedroom and to the one Arlette and I shared. *Had* shared. I could see the tears gushing down his waxy-pale face.

'Put it on the dresser.'

He set the lamp down by the book I had been reading: Sinclair Lewis's *Main Street*. I never finished it; I could never *bear* to finish it. By the light of the lamp, I pointed out the splashes of blood on the floor, and the pool of it right beside the bed.

'More is running out of the quilt,' he said. 'If I'd known how much blood she had in her . . .'

I shook the case free of my pillow and snugged it over the end of the quilt like a sock over a bleeding shin. 'Take her feet,' I said. 'We need to do this part right now. And don't faint again, Henry, because I can't do it by myself.'

'I wish it was a dream,' he said, but he bent and got his arms around the bottom of the quilt. 'Do you think it might be a dream, Poppa?'

'We'll think it is, a year from now when it's all behind us.' Part of me actually believed this. 'Quickly, now. Before the pillowcase starts to drip. Or the rest of the quilt.'

We carried her down the hall, across the sitting room, and out through the front door like men carrying a piece of furniture wrapped in a mover's rug. Once we were down the porch steps, I breathed a little easier; blood in the dooryard could easily be covered over.

Henry was all right until we got around the corner of the cow barn and the old well came in view. It was ringed by wooden stakes so no one would by accident step on the wooden cap that covered it. Those sticks looked grim and horrible in the starlight, and at the sight of them, Henry uttered a strangled cry.

'That's no grave for a mum . . . muh . . .' He managed that much, and then fainted into the weedy scrub that grew behind the barn. Suddenly I was holding the dead weight of my murdered wife all by myself. I considered putting the grotesque bundle down – its wrappings now all askew and the slashed hand peeking out – long enough to revive him. I decided it would be more merciful to let him lie. I dragged her to the side of the well, put her down, and lifted up the wooden cap. As I leaned it against two of the stakes, the well exhaled into my face: a stench of stagnant water and rotting weeds. I fought with my gorge and lost. Holding onto two of the stakes to keep my balance, I bowed at the waist to vomit my supper and the little wine I had drunk. There was an echoing splash when it struck the murky water at the bottom. That splash, like thinking *Ride 'em, Cowboy*, has been within a hand's reach of my memory for the last eight years. I will wake up in the middle of the night with the echo in my mind and feel the splinters of the stakes dig into my palms as I clutch them, holding on for dear life.

I backed away from the well and tripped over the bundle that held Arlette. I fell down. The slashed hand was inches from my eyes. I tucked it back into the quilt and then patted it, as if comforting her. Henry was still lying in the weeds with his head pillowed on one arm. He looked like a child sleeping after a strenuous day during harvest-time. Overhead, the stars shone down in their thousands and tens of thousands. I could see the constellations – Orion, Cassiopeia, the Dippers – that my father had taught me. In the distance, the Cotteries' dog Rex barked once and then was still. I remember thinking, *This night will never end*. And that was right. In all the important ways, it never has.

I picked the bundle up in my arms, and it twitched.

I froze, my breath held in spite of my thundering heart. *Surely I didn't feel that*, I thought. I waited for it to come again. Or perhaps for her hand to creep out of the quilt and try to grip my wrist with the slashed fingers.

There was nothing. I had imagined it. Surely I had. And so I tupped her down the well. I saw the quilt unravel from the end not held by the pillow case, and then came the splash. A much bigger one than my vomit had made, but there was also a squelchy *thud*. I'd known the water down there wasn't deep, but had hoped it would be deep enough to cover her. That thud told me it wasn't.

A high siren of laughter commenced behind me, a sound so close to insanity that it made gooseflesh prickle all the way from the crack of my backside to the nape of my neck. Henry had come to and gained his feet. No, much more than that. He was capering behind the cow barn, waving his arms at the star-shot sky, and laughing.

'Mama down the well and I don't care!' he sing-songed. 'Mama down the well and I don't care, for my master's gone *aw-aaay*!'

I reached him in three strides and slapped him as hard as I could, leaving bloody finger-marks on a downy cheek that hadn't yet felt the stroke of a razor. 'Shut up! Your voice will carry! Your—. There, fool boy, you've raised that God damned dog again.'

Rex barked once, twice, three times. Then silence. We stood, me grasping Henry's shoulders, listening with my head cocked. Sweat ran down the back of my neck. Rex barked once more, then quit. If any of the Cotteries roused, they'd think it was a raccoon he'd been barking at. Or so I hoped.

'Go in the house,' I said. 'The worst is over.'

'Is it, Poppa?' He looked at me solemnly. 'Is it?'

'Yes. Are you all right? Are you going to faint again?'

'Did I?'

'Yes.'

'I'm all right. I just . . . I don't know why I laughed like that. I was confused. Because I'm relieved, I guess. It's over!' A chuckle escaped him, and he clapped his hands over his mouth like a little boy who has inadvertently said a bad word in front of his grandma.

'Yes,' I said. 'It's over. We'll stay here. Your mother ran away to St Louis . . . or perhaps it was Chicago . . . but we'll stay here.'

'She . . . ?' His eyes strayed to the well, and the cap

leaning against three of those stakes that were somehow
so grim in the starlight.

'Yes, Hank, she did.' His mother hated to hear me
call him Hank, she said it was common, but there was
nothing she could do about it now. 'Up and left us cold.
And of course we're sorry, but in the meantime, chores
won't wait. Nor schooling.'

'And I can still be . . . friends with Shannon.'

'Of course,' I said, and in my mind's eye I saw Arlette's
middle finger tapping its lascivious circle around her
crotch. 'Of course you can. But if you should ever feel
the urge to *confess* to Shannon—'

An expression of horror dawned on his face. 'Not
ever!'

'That's what you think now, and I'm glad. But if the
urge should come on you someday, remember this: she'd
run from you.'

'Acourse she would,' he muttered.

'Now go in the house and get both wash-buckets
out of the pantry. Better get a couple of milk-buckets
from the barn, as well. Fill them from the kitchen pump
and suds 'em up with that stuff she keeps under the sink.'

'Should I heat the water?'

I heard my mother say, *Cold water for blood, Wilf.
Remember that.*

'No need,' I said. 'I'll be in as soon as I've put the
cap back on the well.'

He started to turn away, then seized my arm. His
hands were dreadfully cold. 'No one can ever know!' He
whispered this hoarsely into my face. 'No one can ever
know what we did!'

'No one ever will,' I said, sounding far bolder than
I felt. Things had already gone wrong, and I was starting
to realize that a deed is never like the dream of a deed.

'She won't come back, will she?'

'*What?*'

'She won't haunt us, will she?' Only he said *haint*, the kind of country talk that had always made Arlette shake her head and roll her eyes. It is only now, eight years later, that I had come to realize how much *haint* sounds like *hate*.

'No,' I said.

But I was wrong.

I looked down the well, and although it was only 20 feet deep, there was no moon and all I could see was the pale blur of the quilt. Or perhaps it was the pillowcase. I lowered the cover into place, straightened it a little, then walked back to the house. I tried to follow the path we'd taken with our terrible bundle, purposely scuffing my feet, trying to obliterate any traces of blood. I'd do a better job in the morning.

I discovered something that night that most people never have to learn: murder is sin, murder is damnation (surely of one's own mind and spirit, even if the atheists are right and there is no afterlife), but murder is also work. We scrubbed the bedroom until our backs were sore, then moved on to the hall, the sitting room, and finally the porch. Each time we thought we were done, one of us would find another splotch. As dawn began to lighten the sky in the east, Henry was on his knees scrubbing the cracks between the boards of the bedroom floor, and I was down on mine in the sitting room, examining Arlette's hooked rug square inch by square inch, looking for that one drop of blood that might betray us. There was none there – we had been fortunate in that respect – but a dime-sized drop beside it. It looked like blood from a shaving cut. I cleaned it up, then went back into our bedroom to see how Henry was faring. He seemed better now, and I felt better myself. I think it was the coming of daylight, which always seems to dispel the worst of our horrors. But when George, our rooster, let out his first lusty crow of the day, Henry jumped. Then he laughed. It was a small laugh, and there was still something wrong with it, but it didn't terrify me the way his laughter had done when he regained consciousness between the barn and the old livestock well.

'I can't go to school today, Poppa. I'm too tired. And . . . I think people might see it on my face. Shannon especially.'

I hadn't even considered school, which was another sign of half-planning. Half-*assed* planning. I should have put the deed off until County School was out for the summer. It would only have meant waiting a week. 'You can stay home until Monday, then tell the teacher you had the grippe and didn't want to spread it to the rest of the class.'

'It's not the grippe, but I *am* sick.'

So was I.

We had spread a clean sheet from her linen closet (so many things in that house were *hers* . . . but no more) and piled the bloody bedclothes onto it. The mattress was also bloody, of course, and would have to go. There was another, not so good, in the back sheds. I bundled the bedclothes together, and Henry carried the mattress. We went back out to the well just before the sun cleared the horizon. The sky above was perfectly clear. It was going to be a good day for corn.

'I can't look in there, Poppa.'

'You don't have to,' I said, and once more lifted the wooden cover. I was thinking that I should have left it up to begin with – *think ahead, save chores*, my own poppa used to say – and knowing that I never could have. Not after feeling (or thinking I felt) that last blind twitch.

Now I could see to the bottom, and what I saw was horrible. She had landed sitting up with her legs crushed beneath her. The pillowcase was split open and lay in her lap. The quilt and counterpane had come loose and were spread around her shoulders like a complicated ladies' stole. The burlap bag, caught around her head and holding her hair back like a snood, completed the picture: she almost looked as if she were dressed for a night on the town.

Yes! A night on the town! That's why I'm so happy! That's why I'm grinning from ear to ear! And do you notice how red my lipstick is, Wilf? I'd never wear this shade to church, would I? No, this is the kind of lipstick a woman puts on when she wants to do that nasty thing to her man. Come on down, Wilf, why don't you? Don't bother with the ladder, just jump! Show me how bad you want me! You did a nasty thing to me, now let me do one to you!

'Poppa?' Henry was standing with his face toward the barn and his shoulders hunched, like a boy expecting to be beaten. 'Is everything all right?'

'Yes.' I flung down the bundle of linen, hoping it would land on top of her and cover that awful upturned grin, but a whim of draft floated it into her lap, instead. Now she appeared to be sitting in some strange and bloodstained cloud.

'Is she covered? Is she covered up, Poppa?'

I grabbed the mattress and tupped it in. It landed on end in the mucky water and then fell against the circular stone-cobbled wall, making a little lean-to shelter over her, at last hiding her cocked-back head and bloody grin.

'Now she is.' I lowered the old wooden cap back into place, knowing there was more work ahead: the well would have to be filled in. Ah, but that was long overdue, anyway. It was a danger, which was why I had planted the circle of stakes around it. 'Let's go in the house and have breakfast.'

'I couldn't eat a single bite!'

But he did. We both did. I fried eggs, bacon, and

potatoes, and we ate every bite. Hard work makes a person hungry. Everyone knows that.

Henry slept until late afternoon. I stayed awake. Some of those hours I spent at the kitchen table, drinking cup after cup of black coffee. Some of them I spent walking in the corn, up one row and down another, listening to the swordlike leaves rattle in a light breeze. When it's June and corn's on the come, it seems almost to talk. This disquiets some people (and there are the foolish ones who say it's the sound of the corn actually growing), but I had always found that quiet rustling a comfort. It cleared my mind. Now, sitting in this city hotel room, I miss it. City life is no life for a country man; for such a man that life is a kind of damnation in itself.

Confessing, I find, is also hard work.

I walked, I listened to the corn, I tried to plan, and at last I *did* plan. I had to, and not just for myself.

There had been a time not 20 years before, when a man in my position needn't have worried; in those days, a man's business was his own, especially if he happened to be a respected farmer: a fellow who paid his taxes, went to church on Sundays, supported the Hemingford Stars baseball team, and voted the straight Republican ticket. I think that in those days, all sorts of things happened on farms out in what we called 'the middle.' Things that went unremarked, let alone reported. In those days, a man's wife was considered a man's business, and if she disappeared, there was an end to it.

But those days were gone, and even if they hadn't been . . . there was the land. The 100 acres. The Farrington Company wanted those acres for their God damned hog butchery, and Arlette had led them to believe they were going to get them. That meant danger, and danger meant that daydreams and half-plans would no longer suffice.

When I went back to the house at mid-afternoon, I was tired but clear-headed and calm at last. Our few cows were bellowing, their morning milking hours overdue. I did that chore, then put them to pasture where I'd let them stay until sunset, instead of herding them back in for their second milking just after supper. They didn't care; cows accept what *is*. If Arlette had been more like one of our bossies, I reflected, she would still be alive and nagging me for a new washing machine out of the Monkey Ward catalogue. I probably would have bought it for her, too. She could always talk me around. Except when it came to the land. About that she should have known better. Land is a man's business.

Henry was still sleeping. In the weeks that followed, he slept a great deal, and I let him, although in an ordinary summer I would have filled his days with chores once school let out. And he would have filled his evenings either visiting over at Cotteries' or walking up and down our dirt road with Shannon, the two of them holding hands and watching the moon rise. When they weren't kissing, that was. I hoped what we'd done had not spoiled such sweet pastimes for him, but believed it had. That *I* had. And of course I was right.

I cleared my mind of such thoughts, telling myself it was enough for now that he was sleeping. I had to make another visit to the well, and it would be best to do it alone. Our stripped bed seemed to shout murder. I went to the closet and studied her clothes. Women have so many, don't they? Skirts and dresses and blouses and sweaters and underthings – some of the latter so complicated and strange a man can't even tell which side is the front. To take them all would be a mistake, because the truck was still parked in the barn and the Model T under the elm. She had left on foot and taken only what she could carry. Why hadn't she taken the T? Because I would have heard it start and stopped her going. That was believable enough. So . . . a single valise.

I packed it with what I thought a woman would need and what she could not bear to leave. I put in her few pieces of good jewelry and the gold-framed picture of her mama and poppa. I debated over the toiletries in the bathroom, and decided to leave everything except for her atomizer bottler of Florient perfume and her horn-backed brush. There was a Testament in her night table, given to her by Pastor Hawkins, but *I* had never seen her read it, and so left it where it was. But I took the bottle of iron pills, which she kept for her monthlies.

Henry was still sleeping, but now tossing from side to side as if in the grip of bad dreams. I hurried about my business as quickly as I could, wanting to be in the house when he woke up. I went around the barn to the well, put the valise down, and lifted the splintery old cap for the third time. Thank God Henry wasn't with me. Thank God he didn't see what I saw. I think it would have driven him insane. It almost drove me insane.

The mattress had been shunted aside. My first thought was that she had pushed it away before trying to climb out. Because she was still alive. She was breathing. Or so it seemed to me at first. Then, just as ratiocinative ability began to resurface through my initial shock — when I began to ask myself what sort of breathing might cause a woman's dress to rise and fall not just at the bosom but all the way from neckline to hem — her jaw began to move, as if she were struggling to talk. It was not words that emerged from her greatly enlarged mouth, however, but the rat which had been chewing on the delicacy of her tongue. Its tail appeared first. Then her lower jaw yawned wider as it backed out, the claws on its back feet digging into her chin for purchase.

The rat plopped into her lap, and when it did, a

great flood of its brothers and sisters poured out from under her dress. One had something white caught in its whiskers – a fragment of her slip, or perhaps her skimmies. I chucked the valise at them. I didn't think about it – my mind was roaring with revulsion and horror – but just did it. It landed on her legs. Most of the rodents – perhaps all – avoided it nimbly enough. Then they streamed into a round black hole that the mattress (which they must have pushed aside through sheer weight of numbers) had covered, and were gone in a trice. I knew well enough what that hole was; the mouth of the pipe that had supplied water to the troughs in the barn until the water level sank too low and rendered it useless.

Her dress collapsed around her. The counterfeit breathing stopped. But she was *staring* at me, and what had seemed a clown's grin now looked like a gorgon's glare. I could see rat-bites on her cheeks, and one of her earlobes was gone.

'Dear God,' I whispered. 'Arlette, I'm so sorry.'

Your apology is not accepted, her glare seemed to say. *And when they find me like this, with rat-bites on my dead face and the underwear beneath my dress chewed away, you'll ride the lightning over in Lincoln for sure. And mine will be the last face you see. You'll see me when the electricity fries your liver and sets fire to your heart, and I'll be grinning.*

I lowered the cap and staggered to the barn. There my legs betrayed me, and if I'd been in the sun, I surely would have passed out the way Henry had the night before. But I was in the shade, and after I sat for five minutes with my head lowered almost to my knees, I began to feel myself again. The rats had gotten to her – so what? Don't they get to all of us in the end? The rats and bugs? Sooner or later even the stoutest coffin must collapse and let in life to feed on death. It's the way of the world, and what did it matter? When the heart stops and the brain asphyxiates, our spirits either go somewhere else, or simply wink out. Either way, we aren't there to feel the gnawing as our flesh is eaten from our bones.

I started for the house and had reached the porch steps before a thought stopped me: what about the twitch? What if she had been alive when I threw her into the well? What if she had *still* been alive, paralyzed, unable to move so much as one of her slashed fingers, when the rats came out of the pipe and began their depredations? What if she had felt the one that had squirmed into her conveniently enlarged mouth and began to—!

'No,' I whispered. 'She didn't feel it because she didn't twitch. Never did. She was dead when I threw her in.'

'Poppa?' Henry called in a sleep-muzzy voice. 'Pop, is that you?'

'Yes.'

'Who are you talking to?'

'No one. Myself.'

I went in. He was sitting at the kitchen table in his singlet and undershorts, looking dazed and unhappy. His hair, standing up in cowlicks, reminded me of the tyke he had once been, laughing and chasing the chickens around the dooryard with his hound dog Boo (long dead by that summer) at his heels.

'I wish we hadn't done it,' he said as I sat down opposite him.

'Done is done and can't be undone,' I said. 'How many times have I told you that, boy?'

''Bout a million.' He lowered his head for a few moments, then looked up at me. His eyes were red-rimmed and bloodshot. 'Are we going to be caught? Are we going to jail? Or . . .'

'No. I've got a plan.'

'You had a plan that it wouldn't hurt her! Look how *that* turned out!'

My hand itched to slap him for that, so I held it down with the other. This was not the time for recriminations. Besides, he was right. Everything that had gone wrong was my fault. *Except for the rats*, I thought. *They are not my fault.* But they were. Of course they were. If not for me, she would have been at the stove, putting on supper. Probably going on and on about those 100 acres, yes, but alive and well instead of *in* the well.

The rats are probably back already, a voice deep in my mind whispered. *Eating her. They'll finish the good parts, the tasty parts, the* delicacies, *and then . . .*

Henry reached across the table to touch my knotted hands. I started.

'I'm sorry,' he said. 'We're in it together.'

I loved him for that.

'We're going to be all right, Hank; if we keep our heads, we'll be fine. Now listen to me.'

He listened. At some point he began to nod. When I finished, he asked me one question: when were we going to fill in the well?

'Not yet,' I said.

'Isn't that risky?'

'Yes,' I said.

Two days later, while I was mending a piece of fence about a quarter-mile from the farm, I saw a large cloud of dust boiling down our road from the Omaha-Lincoln Highway. We were about to have a visit from the world that Arlette had so badly wanted to be a part of. I walked back to the house with my hammer tucked into a belt loop and my carpenter's apron around my waist, its long pouch full of jingling nails. Henry was not in view. Perhaps he'd gone down to the spring to bathe; perhaps he was in his room, sleeping.

By the time I got to the dooryard and sat on the

chopping block, I had recognized the vehicle pulling the rooster-tail: Lars Olsen's Red Baby delivery truck. Lars was the Hemingford Home blacksmith and village milkman. He would also, for a price, serve as a kind of chauffeur, and it was that function he was fulfilling on this June afternoon. The truck pulled into the dooryard, putting George, our bad-tempered rooster, and his little harem of chickens to flight. Before the motor had even finished coughing itself to death, a portly man wrapped in a flapping gray duster got out on the passenger side. He pulled off his goggles to reveal large (and comical) white circles around his eyes.

'Wilfred James?'

'At your service,' I said, getting up. I felt calm enough. I might have felt less so if he'd come out in the county Ford with the star on the side. 'You are—?'

'Andrew Lester,' he said. 'Attorney-at-law.'

He put his hand out. I considered it.

'Before I shake that, you'd better tell me whose lawyer you are, Mr Lester.'

'I'm currently being retained by the Farrington Livestock Company of Chicago, Omaha, and Des Moines.'

Yes, I thought, *I've no doubt. But I'll bet your name isn't even on the door. The big boys back in Omaha don't have to eat country dust to pay for their daily bread, do they? The big boys have got their feet up on their desks, drinking coffee and admiring the pretty ankles of their secretaries.*

I said, 'In that case, sir, why don't you just go on and put that hand away? No offense.'

He did just that, and with a lawyer's smile. Sweat was cutting clean lines down his chubby cheeks, and his hair was all matted and tangled from the ride. I walked past him to Lars, who had thrown up the wing over his engine and was fiddling with something inside. He was whistling and sounded just as happy as a bird on a wire.

I envied him that. I thought Henry and I might have another happy day – in a world as varied as this one, anything is possible – but it would not be in the summer of 1922. Or the fall.

I shook Lars's hand and asked how he was.

'Tolerable fair,' he said, 'but dry. I could use a drink.'

I nodded toward the east side of the house. 'You know where it is.'

'I do,' he said, slamming down the wing with a metallic clatter that sent the chickens, who'd been creeping back, into flight once more. 'Sweet and cold as ever, I guess?'

'I'd say so,' I agreed, thinking: *But if you could still pump from that other well, Lars, I don't think you'd care for the taste at all.* 'Try it and see.'

He started around to the shady side of the house where the outside pump stood in its little shelter. Mr Lester watched him go, then turned back to me. He had unbuttoned his duster. The suit beneath would need dry-cleaning when he got back to Lincoln, Omaha, Deland, or wherever he hung his hat when he wasn't doing Cole Farrington's business.

'I could use a drink myself, Mr James.'

'Me, too. Nailing fence is hot work.' I looked him up and down. 'Not as hot as riding twenty miles in Lars's truck, though, I'll bet.'

He rubbed his butt and smiled his lawyer's smile. This time it had a touch of rue in it. I could see his eyes already flicking here, there, and everywhere. It would not do to sell this man short just because he'd been ordered to rattle twenty miles out into the country on a hot summer's day. 'My sit-upon may never be the same.'

There was a dipper chained to the side of the little shelter. Lars pumped it full, drank it down with his Adam's apple rising and falling in his scrawny, sunburned neck, then filled it again and offered it to Lester, who looked at it as doubtfully as I'd looked at his outstretched hand. 'Perhaps we could drink it inside, Mr James. It would be a little cooler.'

'It would,' I agreed, 'but I'd no more invite you inside than I'd shake your hand.'

Lars Olsen saw how the wind was blowing and wasted no time going back to his truck. But he handed the dipper to Lester first. My visitor didn't drink in gulps, as Lars had, but in fastidious sips. Like a lawyer, in other words – but he didn't stop until the dipper was empty, and that was also like a lawyer. The screen door slammed and Henry came out of the house in his overalls and bare feet. He gave us a glance that seemed utterly disinterested – good boy! – and then went where any red-blooded country lad would have gone: to watch Lars work on his truck, and, if he were lucky, to learn something.

I sat down on the woodpile we kept under a swatch of canvas on this side of the house. 'I imagine you're out here on business. My wife's.'

'I am.'

'Well, you've had your drink, so we better get down to it. I've still got a full day's work ahead of me, and it's three in the afternoon.'

'Sunrise to sunset. Farming's a hard life.' He sighed as if he knew.

'It is, and a difficult wife can make it even harder. She sent you, I suppose, but I don't know why – if it was just some legal paperwork, I reckon a sheriff's deputy would have come out and served it on me.'

He looked at me in surprise. 'Your wife didn't send me, Mr James. In point of fact, I came out here to look for *her*.'

It was like a play, and this was my cue to look puzzled. Then to chuckle, because chuckling came next in the stage directions. 'That just proves it.'

'Proves what?'

'When I was a boy in Fordyce, we had a neighbor – a nasty old rip name of Bradlee. Everyone called him Pop Bradlee.'

'Mr James—'

'My father had to do business with him from time to time, and sometimes he took me with him. Back in the buckboard days, this was. Seed corn was what their trading was mostly about, at least in the spring, but sometimes they also swapped tools. There was no mail-order back then, and a good tool might circle the whole county before it got back home.'

'Mr James, I hardly see the rel—'

'And every time we went to see that old fellow, my mama told me to plug my ears, because every other word that came out of Pop Bradlee's mouth was a cuss or something filthy.' In a sour sort of way, I was starting to enjoy this. 'So naturally I listened all the harder. I remember that one of Pop's favorite sayings was "Never mount a mare without a bridle, because you can never tell which way a bitch will run."'

'Am I supposed to understand that?'

'Which way do you suppose *my* bitch ran, Mr Lester?'

'Are you telling me your wife has . . . ?'

'Absconded, Mr Lester. Decamped. Took French leave. Did a midnight flit. As an avid reader and student of American slang, such terms occur naturally to me. Lars, however – and most other town folks – will just say "She run off and left him" when the word gets around. Or him and the boy, in this case. I naturally thought she would have gone to her hog-fancying friends at the Farrington Company, and the next I heard from her would have been a notice that she was selling her father's acreage.'

'As she means to do.'

'Has she signed it over yet? Because I guess I'd have to go to law, if she has.'

'As a matter of fact, she hasn't. But when she does, I would advise you against the expense of a legal action you would surely lose.'

I stood up. One of my overall straps had fallen off my shoulder, and I hooked it back into place with a thumb. 'Well, since she's not here, it's what the legal profession calls "a moot question," wouldn't you say? I'd look in Omaha, if I were you.' I smiled. 'Or Saint Louis. She was *always* talking about Sain'-Loo. It sounds to me as if she got as tired of you fellows as she did of me and the son she gave birth to. Said good riddance to bad rubbish. A plague on both your houses. That's Shakespeare, by the way. *Romeo and Juliet.* A play about love.'

'You'll pardon me for saying, but all this seems very strange to me, Mr James.' He had produced a silk handkerchief from a pocket inside his suit – I bet traveling lawyers like him have lots of pockets – and began to mop his face with it. His cheeks were now not just flushed but bright red. It wasn't the heat of the day that had turned his face that color. 'Very strange indeed, considering the amount of money my client is willing to pay for that piece of property, which is contiguous with Hemingford Stream and close to the Great Western rail line.'

'It's going to take some getting used to on my part as well, but I have the advantage of you.'

'Yes?'

'I know her. I'm sure you and your *clients* thought you had a deal all made, but Arlette James . . . let's just say that nailing her down to something is like trying to nail jelly to the floor. We need to remember what Pop Bradlee said, Mr Lester. Why, the man was a countrified genius.'

'Could I look in the house?'

I laughed again, and this time it wasn't forced. The

man had gall, I'll give him that, and not wanting to go back empty-handed was understandable. He'd ridden twenty miles in a dusty truck with no doors, he had twenty more to bounce across before he got back to Hemingford City (and a train ride after that, no doubt), he had a sore ass, and the people who'd sent him out here weren't going to be happy with his report when he finally got to the end of all that hard traveling. Poor feller!

'I'll ask you one back: could you drop your pants so I could look at your goolie-bits?'

'I find that offensive.'

'I don't blame you. Think of it as a . . . not a simile, that's not right, but a kind of *parable*.'

'I don't understand you.'

'Well, you've got an hour back to the city to think it over — two, if Lars's Red Baby throws a tire. And I can assure you, Mr Lester, that if I *did* let you poke around through my house — my private place, my castle, my goolie-bits — you wouldn't find my wife's body in the closet or . . .' There was a terrible moment when I almost said *or down the well*. I felt sweat spring out on my forehead. 'Or under the bed.'

'I never said—'

'Henry!' I called. 'Come over here a minute!'

Henry came with his head down and his feet dragging in the dust. He looked worried, maybe even guilty, but that was all right. 'Yes, sir?'

'Tell this man where's your mama.'

'I don't know. When you called me to breakfast Friday morning, she was gone. Packed and gone.'

Lester was looking at him keenly. 'Son, is that the truth?'

'Yes, sir.'

'The whole truth and nothing *but* the truth, so help you God?'

'Poppa, can I go back in the house? I've got school-work to make up from being sick.'

'Go on, then,' I said, 'but don't be slow. Remember, it's your turn to milk.'

'Yes, sir.'

He trudged up the steps and inside. Lester watched him go, then turned back to me. 'There's more here than meets the eye.'

'I see you wear no wedding ring, Mr Lester. If there comes a time when you've worn one as long as I have, you'll know that in families, there always is. And you'll know something else as well: you can never tell which way a bitch will run.'

He got up. 'This isn't finished.'

'It is,' I said. Knowing it wasn't. But if things went all right, we were closer to the end than we had been. *If.*

He started across the dooryard, then turned back. He used his silk handkerchief to mop off his face again, then said, 'If you think those 100 acres are yours just because you've scared your wife away . . . sent her packing to her aunt in Des Moines or a sister in Minnesota—'

'Check Omaha,' I said, smiling. 'Or Sain'-Loo. She had no use for her relations, but she was crazy about the idea of living in Sain'-Loo. God knows why.'

'If you think you'll plant and harvest out there, you'd better think again. That land's not yours. If you so much as drop a seed there, you will be seeing me in court.'

I said, 'I'm sure you'll hear from her as soon as she gets a bad case of broke-itis.'

What I wanted to say was, *No, it's not mine . . . but it's not yours, either. It's just going to sit there. And that's all right, because it* will *be mine in seven years, when I go to court to have her declared legally dead. I can wait. Seven years without smelling pigshit when the wind's out of the west? Seven years without hearing the screams of dying hogs (so much like the screams of a dying woman) or seeing their intestines float down a creek that's red with blood? That sounds like an excellent seven years to me.*

'Have yourself a fine day, Mr Lester, and mind the sun going back. It gets pretty fierce in the late afternoon, and it'll be right in your face.'

He got into the truck without replying. Lars waved to me and Lester snapped at him. Lars gave him a look that might have meant *Snap and yap all you want, it's still twenty miles back to Hemingford City.*

When they were gone except for the rooster-tail of dust, Henry came back out on the porch. 'Did I do it right, Poppa?'

I took his wrist, gave it a squeeze, and pretended not to feel the flesh tighten momentarily under my hand, as if he had to override an impulse to pull away. 'Just right. Perfect.'

'Are we going to fill in the well tomorrow?'

I thought about this carefully, because our lives might depend on what I decided. Sheriff Jones was getting on in years and up in pounds. He wasn't lazy, but it was hard to get him moving without a good reason. Lester would eventually convince Jones to come out here, but probably not until Lester got one of Cole Farrington's two hell-for-leather sons to call and remind the Sheriff what company was the biggest taxpayer in Hemingford County (not to mention the neighboring counties of Clay, Fillmore, York, and Seward). Still, I thought we had at least two days.

'Not tomorrow,' I said. 'The day after.'

'Poppa, *why*?'

'Because the High Sheriff will be out here, and Sheriff Jones is old but not stupid. A filled-in well might make him suspicious about *why* it got filled in, so recent and all. But one that's still *being* filled in . . . and for a good reason . . .'

'What reason? Tell me!'
'Soon,' I said. 'Soon.'

All the next day we waited to see dust boiling toward us down our road, not being pulled by Lars Olsen's truck but by the County Sheriff's car. It didn't come. What came was Shannon Cotterie, looking pretty in a cotton blouse and gingham skirt, to ask if Henry was all right, and could he take supper with her and her mama and her poppa if he was?

Henry said he was fine, and I watched them go up the road, hand-in-hand, with deep misgivings. He was keeping a terrible secret, and terrible secrets are heavy. Wanting to share them is the most natural thing in the world. And he loved the girl (or thought he did, which comes to the same when you're just going on 15). To make things worse, he had a lie to tell, and she might know it was a lie. They say that loving eyes can never see, but that's a fool's axiom. Sometimes they see too much.

I hoed in the garden (pulling up more peas than weeds), then sat on the porch, smoking a pipe and waiting for him to come back. Just before moonrise, he did. His head was down, his shoulders were slumped, and he was trudging rather than walking. I hated to see him that way, but I was still relieved. If he had shared his secret – or even part of it – he wouldn't have been walking like that. If he'd shared his secret, he might not have come back at all.

'You told it the way we decided?' I asked him when he sat down.

'The way *you* decided. Yes.'

'And she promised not to tell her folks?'

'Yes.'

'But will she?'

He sighed. 'Probably, yes. She loves them and they love her. They'll see something in her face, I reckon, and get it out of her. And even if they don't, she'll probably tell the Sheriff. If he bothers to talk to the Cotteries at all, that is.'

'Lester will see that he does. He'll bark at Sheriff Jones because his bosses in Omaha are barking at him. Round and round it goes, and where it stops, nobody knows.'

'We never should have done it.' He considered, then said it again in a fierce whisper.

I said nothing. For awhile, neither did he. We watched the moon rise out of the corn, red and pregnant.

'Poppa? Can I have a glass of beer?'

I looked at him, surprised and not surprised. Then I went inside and poured us each a glass of beer. I gave one to him and said, 'None of this tomorrow or the day after, mind.'

'No.' He sipped, grimaced, then sipped again. 'I hated lying to Shan, Poppa. Everything about this is dirty.'

'Dirt washes off.'

'Not this kind,' he said, and took another sip. This time he didn't grimace.

A little while later, after the moon had gone to silver, I stepped around to use the privy, and to listen to the corn and the night breeze tell each other the old secrets of the earth. When I got back to the porch, Henry was gone. His glass of beer stood half-finished on the railing by the steps. Then I heard him in the barn, saying 'Soo, Boss. Soo.'

I went out to see. He had his arms around Elphis's neck and was stroking her. I believe he was crying. I watched for awhile, but in the end said nothing. I went back to the house, undressed, and lay down in the bed where I'd cut my wife's throat. It was a long time before I went to sleep. And if you don't understand why – *all* the reasons why – then reading this is of no use to you.

★   ★   ★

I had named all our cows after minor Greek goddesses, but Elphis turned out to be either a bad choice or an ironic joke. In case you don't remember the story of how evil came to our sad old world, let me refresh you: all the bad things flew out when Pandora gave in to her curiosity and opened the jar that had been left in her keeping. The only thing that remained when she regained enough wits to put the lid back on was Elphis, the goddess of hope. But in that summer of 1922, there was no hope left for our Elphis. She was old and cranky, no longer gave much milk, and we'd all but given up trying to get what little she had; as soon as you sat down on the stool, she'd try to kick you. We should have converted her into comestibles a year before, but I balked at the cost of having Harlan Cotterie butcher her, and I was no good at slaughtering much beyond hogs . . . a self-assessment with which you, Reader, must now surely agree.

'And she'd be tough,' Arlette (who had shown a sneaking affection for Elphis, perhaps because she was never the one to milk her) said. 'Better leave well enough alone.' But now we had a use for Elphis – *in* the well, as it so happened – and her death might serve an end far more useful than a few stringy cuts of meat.

Two days after Lester's visit, my son and I put a nose-halter on her and led her around the side of the barn. Halfway to the well, Henry stopped. His eyes shone with dismay. 'Poppa! I *smell* her!'

'Go into the house then, and get some cotton balls for your nose. They're on her dresser.'

Although his head was lowered, I saw the sidelong glance he shot me as he went. *This is all your fault*, that look said. *All your fault because you couldn't let go.*

Yet I had no doubt that he would help me do the work that lay ahead. Whatever he now thought of me, there was a girl in the picture as well, and he didn't want her to know what he had done. I had forced him to it, but she would never understand that.

We led Elphis to the well-cap, where she quite reasonably balked. We went around to the far side, holding the halter-strings like ribbons in a Maypole dance, and hauled her out onto the rotted wood by main force. The cap cracked beneath her weight . . . bowed down . . . but held. The old cow stood on it, head lowered, looking as stupid and as stubborn as ever, showing the greenish-yellow rudiments of her teeth.

'What now?' Henry asked.

I started to say I didn't know, and that was when the well-cap broke in two with a loud and brittle snap. We held onto the halter-strings, although I thought for a moment I was going to be dragged into that damned well with two dislocated arms. Then the nose-rig ripped free and flew back up. It was split down both the sides. Below, Elphis began to low in agony and drum her hoofs against the well's rock sides.

'*Poppa!*' Henry screamed. His hands were fists against his mouth, the knuckles digging into his upper lip. '*Make her stop!*'

Elphis uttered a long, echoing groan. Her hoofs continued to beat against the stone.

I took Henry's arm and hauled him, stumbling, back to the house. I pushed him down on Arlette's mail-order sofa and ordered him to stay there until I came back to get him. 'And remember, this is almost over.'

'It'll never be over,' he said, and turned facedown on the sofa. He put his hands over his ears, even though Elphis couldn't be heard from in here. Except Henry still *was* hearing her, and so was I.

I got my varmint gun from the high shelf in the pantry. It was only a .22, but it would do the job. And if Harlan heard shots rolling across the acres between his place and mine? That would fit our story, too. If Henry could keep his wits long enough to tell it, that was.

Here is something I learned in 1922: there are always worse things waiting. You think you have seen the most terrible thing, the one that coalesces all your nightmares into a freakish horror that actually exists, and the only consolation is that there can be nothing worse. Even if there is, your mind will snap at the sight of it, and you will know no more. But there *is* worse, your mind does *not* snap, and somehow you carry on. You might understand that all the joy has gone out of the world for you, that what you did has put all you hoped to gain out of your reach, you might wish you were the one who was dead – but you go on. You realize that you are in a hell of your own making, but you go on nevertheless. Because there is nothing else to do.

Elphis had landed on top of my wife's body, but Arlette's grinning face was still perfectly visible, still tilted up to the sunlit world above, still seeming to look at me. And the rats had come back. The cow falling into their world had doubtless caused them to retreat into the pipe I would eventually come to think of as Rat Boulevard, but then they had smelled fresh meat, and had come hurrying out to investigate. They were already nibbling at poor old Elphis as she lowed and kicked (more feebly now), and one sat on top of my dead wife's head like an eldritch crown. It had picked a hole in the burlap sack and pulled a tuft of her hair out with its clever claws. Arlette's cheeks, once so round and pretty, hung in shreds.

Nothing can be any worse than this, I thought. *Surely I've reached the end of horror.*

But yes, there are always worse things waiting. As I peered down, frozen with shock and revulsion, Elphis kicked out again, and one of her hoofs connected with what remained of Arlette's face. There was a snap as my wife's jaw broke, and everything below her nose shifted to the left, as if on a hinge. Still the ear-to-ear grin remained. That it was no longer aligned with her eyes made it even worse. It was as if she now had two faces to haunt me with instead of just one. Her body shifted against the mattress, making it slide. The rat on her head scurried down behind it. Elphis lowed again. I thought that if Henry came back now, and looked into the well, he would kill me for making him a part of this. I probably deserved killing. But that would leave him alone, and alone he would be defenseless.

Part of the cap had fallen into the well; part of it was still hanging down. I loaded my rifle, rested it on this slope, and aimed at Elphis, who lay with her neck broken and her head cocked against the rock wall. I waited for my hands to steady, then pulled the trigger.

One shot was enough.

Back in the house, I found that Henry had gone to sleep on the couch. I was too shocked myself to consider this strange. At that moment, he seemed to me like the only truly hopeful thing in the world: soiled, but not so filthy he could never be clean again. I bent and kissed his cheek. He moaned and turned his head away. I left him there and went to the barn for my tools. When he joined me three hours later, I had pulled the broken and hanging piece of the well-cap out of the hole and had begun to fill it in.

'I'll help,' he said in a flat and dreary voice.

'Good. Get the truck and drive it out to the dirtpile at West Fence—'

'By myself?' The disbelief in his voice was only faint, but I was encouraged to hear any emotion at all.

'You know all the forward gears, and you can find reverse, can't you?'

'Yes—'

'Then you'll be fine. I've got enough to be going on with in the meantime, and when you come back, the worst will be over.'

I waited for him to tell me again that the worst would never be over, but he didn't. I recommenced shoveling. I could still see the top of Arlette's head and the burlap with that terrible picked-over tuft sticking out of it. There might already be a litter of newborn ratlings down there in the cradle of my dead wife's thighs.

I heard the truck cough once, then twice. I hoped the crank wouldn't kick back and break Henry's arm.

The third time he turned the crank, our old truck bellowed into life. He retarded the spark, gunned the throttle a time or two, then drove away. He was gone for almost an hour, but when he came back, the truck's bed was full of rocks and soil. He drove it to the edge of the well and killed the engine. He had taken off his shirt, and his sweat-shiny torso looked too thin; I could count his ribs. I tried to think when I'd last seen him eat a big meal, and at first I couldn't. Then I realized it must have been breakfast on the morning after we'd done away with her.

I'll see that he gets a good dinner tonight, I thought. *I'll see that we both do. No beef, but there's pork in the icebox—*

'Look yonder,' he said in his new flat voice, and pointed.

I saw a rooster-tail of dust coming toward us. I looked down into the well. It wasn't good enough, not yet. Half of Elphis was still sticking up. That was all right, of course, but the corner of the bloodstained mattress was also still poking out of the dirt.

'Help me,' I said.

'Do we have enough time, Poppa?' He sounded only mildly interested.

'I don't know. Maybe. Don't just stand there, help me.'

The extra shovel was leaning against the side of the

barn beside the splintered remains of the well-cap. Henry grabbed it, and we began shoveling dirt and rocks out of the back of the truck as fast as ever we could.

When the County Sheriff's car with the gold star on the door and the spotlight on the roof pulled up by the chopping block (once more putting George and the chickens to flight), Henry and I were sitting on the porch steps with our shirts off and sharing the last thing Arlette James had ever made: a pitcher of lemonade. Sheriff Jones got out, hitched up his belt, took off his Stetson, brushed back his graying hair, and resettled his hat along the line where the white skin of his brow ended and coppery red took over. He was by his lonesome. I took that as a good sign.

'Good day, gents.' He took in our bare chests, dirty hands, and sweaty faces. 'Hard chorin' this afternoon, is it?'

I spat. 'My own damn fault.'

'Is that so?'

'One of our cows fell in the old livestock well,' Henry said.

Jones asked again, 'Is that so?'

'It is,' I said. 'Would you want a glass of lemonade, Sheriff? It's Arlette's.'

'Arlette's, is it? She decided to come back, did she?'

'No,' I said. 'She took her favorite clothes but left the lemonade. Have some.'

'I will. But first I need to use your privy. Since I turned fifty-five or so, seems like I have to wee on every bush. It's a God damned inconvenience.'

'It's around the back of the house. Just follow the path and look for the crescent moon on the door.'

He laughed as though this were the funniest joke he'd heard all year, and went around the house. Would he pause on his way to look in the windows? He would if he was any good at his job, and I'd heard he was. At least in his younger days.

'Poppa,' Henry said. He spoke in a low voice.

I looked at him.

'If he finds out, we can't do anything else. I can lie, but there can't be anymore killing.'

'All right,' I said. That was a short conversation, but one I have pondered often in the eight years since.

Sheriff Jones came back, buttoning his fly.

'Go in and get the Sheriff a glass,' I told Henry.

Henry went. Jones finished with his fly, took off his hat, brushed back his hair some more, and reset the hat. His badge glittered in the early-afternoon sun. The gun on his hip was a big one, and although Jones was too old to have been in the Great War, the holster looked like AEF property. Maybe it was his son's. His son had died over there.

'Sweet-smelling privy,' he said. 'Always nice on a hot day.'

'Arlette used to put the quicklime to it pretty constantly,' I said. 'I'll try to keep up the practice if she stays away. Come on up to the porch and we'll sit in the shade.'

'Shade sounds good, but I believe I'll stand. Need to stretch out my spine.'

I sat in my rocker with the PA cushion on it. He stood beside me, looking down. I didn't like being in that position but tried to bear up patiently. Henry came out with a glass. Sheriff Jones poured his own lemonade, tasted, then gulped most of it down at a go and smacked his lips.

'Good, isn't it? Not too sour, not too sweet, just right.' He laughed. 'I'm like Goldilocks, aren't I?' He drank the rest, but shook his head when Henry offered to refill his glass. 'You want me pissing on every fencepost on the way back to Hemingford Home? And then all the way to Hemingford City after that?'

'Have you moved your office?' I asked. 'I thought you were right there in the Home.'

'I am, aren't I? The day they make me move the Sheriff's Office to the county seat is the day I resign and let Hap Birdwell take over, like he wants to. No, no, it's just a court hearing up to the City. Amounts to no more than paperwork, but there it is. And you know how Judge Cripps is . . . or no, I guess you don't, being a law-abiding sort. He's bad-tempered, and if a fellow isn't on time, his temper gets worse. So even though it comes down to just saying so help me God and then signing my name to a bunch of legal folderol, I have to hurry right along with my business out here, don't I? And hope my God damned Maxie doesn't break down on the way back.'

I said nothing to this. He didn't *talk* like a man who was in a hurry, but perhaps that was just his way.

He took his hat off and brushed his hair back some more, but this time he didn't put the hat back on. He looked at me earnestly, then at Henry, then back at me again. 'Guess you know I'm not out here on my own hook. I believe that doings between a man and his wife are their own business. It has to be that way, doesn't it? Bible says the man is the head of a woman, and that if a woman should learn any thing, it should be taught by her husband at home. Book of Corinthians. If the Bible was my only boss, I'd do things the Bible's way and life would be simpler.'

'I'm surprised Mr Lester's not out here with you,' I said.

'Oh, he wanted to come, but I put the kye-bosh on that. He also wanted me to get a search warrant, but I told him I didn't need one. I said you'd either let me look around or you wouldn't.' He shrugged. His face was placid, but the eyes were keen and always in motion: peeking and prying, prying and peeking.

When Henry asked me about the well, I'd said, *We'll watch him and decide how sharp he is. If he's sharp, we'll show him ourselves. We can't look as if we have anything to hide. If you see me flick my thumb, that means I think we have to take the chance. But we have to agree, Hank. If I don't see you flick yours back, I'll keep my mouth shut.*

I raised my glass and drank the last of my lemonade. When I saw Henry looking at me, I flicked my thumb. Just a little. It could have been a muscle twitch.

'What does that Lester think?' Henry asked, sounding indignant. 'That we've got her tied up in the cellar?' His own hands stayed at his sides, not moving.

Sheriff Jones laughed heartily, his big belly shaking behind his belt. 'I don't know *what* he's thinking, do I? I don't care much, either. Lawyers are fleas on the hide of human nature. I can say that, because I've worked for 'em – and against 'em, that too – my whole adult life. But . . .' The keen eyes fastened on mine. 'I wouldn't mind a look, just because you wouldn't let *him* look. He's pretty hot under the collar about that.'

Henry scratched his arm. His thumb flicked twice as he did it.

'I didn't let him in the house because I took against him,' I said. 'Although to be fair, I guess I would have taken against John the Apostle if he came out here batting for Cole Farrington's team.'

Sheriff Jones laughed big at that: *Haw, haw, haw!* But his eyes didn't laugh.

I stood up. It was a relief to be on my feet. Standing, I had three or four inches on Jones. 'You can look to your heart's content.'

'I appreciate that. It'll make my life a lot easier, won't it? I've got Judge Cripps to deal with when I go back, and that's enough. Don't need to listen to one of Farrington's legal beagles yapping at me, not if I can help it.'

We went into the house with me leading and Henry bringing up the rear. After a few complimentary remarks about how neat the sitting room was and how tidy the kitchen was, we walked down the hall. Sheriff Jones had a perfunctory peek into Henry's room, and then we arrived at the main attraction. I pushed open the door to our bedroom with a queer sense of certainty: the blood would be back. It would be pooled on the floor, splashed on the walls, and soaking into the new mattress. Sheriff Jones would look. Then he would turn to me, remove the handcuffs that sat on his meaty hip across from his revolver, and say: *I'm arresting you for the murder of Arlette James, aren't I?*

There was no blood and no smell of blood, because the room had had days to air out. The bed was made, although not the way Arlette made it; my way was more Army-style, although my feet had kept me out of the war that had taken the Sheriff's son. Can't go kill Krauts if you have flat feet. Men with flat feet can only kill wives.

'Lovely room,' Sheriff Jones remarked. 'Gets the early light, doesn't it?'

'Yes,' I said. 'And stays cool most afternoons, even in summer, because the sun's over on the other side.' I went to the closet and opened it. That sense of certainty returned, stronger than ever. *Where's the quilt?* he'd say. *The one that belongs there in the middle of the top shelf?*

He didn't, of course, but he came forward with alacrity when I invited him to. His sharp eyes – bright green, almost feline – went here, there, and everywhere. 'Lot o' duds,' he said.

'Yes,' I admitted, 'Arlette liked clothes and she liked the mail-order catalogues. But since she only took the one valise – we have two, and the other one's still there, see it in the back corner? – I'd have to say she only took the ones she liked the best. And the ones that were practical, I suppose. She had two pairs of slacks and a pair of blue denims, and those are gone, even though she didn't care for pants.'

'Pants're good for traveling in, though, aren't they? Man or woman, pants are good for traveling. And a woman might choose them. If she was in a hurry, that is.'

'I suppose.'

'She took her good jewelry and her picture of Nana and Pop-Pop,' Henry said from behind us. I jumped a little; I'd almost forgotten he was there.

'Did she, now? Well, I suppose she would.'

He took another flick through the clothes, then closed the closet door. 'Nice room,' he said, trudging back toward the hall with his Stetson in his hands. 'Nice *house*. Woman'd have to be crazy to leave a nice room and a nice house like this.'

'Mama talked about the city a lot,' Henry said, and sighed. 'She had the idea of opening some kind of shop.'

'Did she?' Sheriff Jones regarded him brightly with his green cat's eyes. 'Well! But a thing like that takes money, doesn't it?'

'She's got those acres from her father,' I said.

'Yes, yes.' Smiling bashfully, as if he'd forgotten those acres. 'And maybe it's for the best. "Better to be living in a wasteland than with a bitter-tongued, angry woman." Book of Proverbs. Are you glad she's gone, Son?'

'No,' Henry said, and tears overspilled his eyes. I blessed each one.

Sheriff Jones said, 'There-there.' And after offering that perfunctory comfort, he bent down with his hands braced on his pudgy knees, and looked under the bed. 'Appears to be a pair of woman's shoes under there. Broke in, too. The kind that would be good for walking. Don't suppose she ran away barefooty, do you?'

'She wore her canvas shoes,' I said. 'Those are the ones that are gone.'

They were, too. The faded green ones she used to call her gardening shoes. I'd remembered them just before starting to fill in the well.

'Ah!' he said. 'Another mystery solved.' He pulled a silver-plated watch from his vest pocket and consulted it. 'Well, I'd better get on the roll. Tempus is fugiting right along.'

We went back through the house, Henry bringing up the rear, perhaps so he could swipe his eyes dry in privacy. We walked with the Sheriff toward his Maxwell sedan with the star on the door. I was about to ask him if he wanted to see the well – I even knew what I was going to call it – when he stopped and gave my son a look of frightening kindness.

'I stopped at the Cotteries',' he said.

'Oh?' Henry said. 'Did you?'

'Told you these days I have to water just about every bush, but I'll use a privy anytime there's one handy, always assuming folks keep it clean and I don't have to worry about wasps while I'm waiting for my dingus to drip a little water. And the Cotteries are clean folks. Pretty daughter, too. Just about your age, isn't she?'

'Yes, sir,' Henry said, lifting his voice just a tiny bit on the *sir*.

'Kind of sweet on her, I guess? And her on you, from what her mama says.'

'Did she say that?' Henry asked. He sounded surprised, but pleased, too.

'Yes. Mrs Cotterie said you were troubled about your own mama, and that Shannon had told her something you said on that subject. I asked her what it was, and she said it wasn't her place to tell, but I could ask Shannon. So I did.'

Henry looked at his feet. 'I told her to keep it to herself.'

'You aren't going to hold it against her, are you?'

Sheriff Jones asked. 'I mean, when a big man like me with a star on his chest asks a little thing like her what she knows, it's kind of hard for the little thing to keep mum, isn't it? She just about has to tell, doesn't she?'

'I don't know,' Henry said, still looking down. 'Probably.' He wasn't just *acting* unhappiness; he *was* unhappy. Even though it was going just the way we had hoped it would.

'Shannon says your ma and your pop here had a big fight about selling those hundred acres, and when you came down on your poppa's side, Missus James slapped you up pretty good.'

'Yes,' Henry said colorlessly. 'She'd had too much to drink.'

Sheriff Jones turned to me. 'Was she drunk or just tiddly?'

'Somewhere in between,' I said. 'If she'd been all the way to drunk, she would have slept all night instead of getting up and packing a grip and creeping away like a thief.'

'Thought she'd come back once she sobered up, did you?'

'I did. It's over four miles out to the tarvy. I thought for sure she'd come back. Someone must have come along and given her a ride before her head cleared. A trucker on the Lincoln–Omaha run would be my guess.'

'Yep, yep, that'd be mine, too. You'll hear from her when she contacts Mr Lester, I'm sure. If she means to stay out on her own, if she's got that in her head, she'll need money to do it.'

So he knew that, too.

His eyes sharpened. 'Did she have any money at all, Mr James?'

'Well . . .'

'Don't be shy. Confession's good for the soul. The Catholics have got hold of something there, don't they?'

'I kept a box in my dresser. There was 200 dollars put by in it, to help pay the pickers when they start next month.'

'And Mr Cotterie,' Henry reminded. To Sheriff Jones, he said: 'Mr Cotterie has a corn harvester. A Harris Giant. Almost new. It's a pip.'

'Yep, yep, saw it in his dooryard. Big bastid, isn't it? Pardon my Polish. Money all gone out'n that box, was it?'

I smiled sourly – only it wasn't really me making that smile; the Conniving Man had been in charge ever since Sheriff Jones pulled up by the chopping block. 'She left twenty. Very generous of her. But twenty's all Harlan Cotterie will ever take for the use of his harvester, so *that's* all right. And when it comes to the pickers, I guess Stoppenhauser at the bank'll advance me a shortie loan. Unless he owes favors to the Farrington Company, that is. Either way, I've got my best farmhand right here.'

I tried to ruffle Henry's hair. He ducked away, embarrassed.

'Well, I've got a good budget of news to tell Mr Lester, don't I? He won't like any of it, but if he's as smart as he thinks he is, I guess he'll know enough to expect her in his office, and sooner rather than later. People have a way of turning up when they're short on folding green, don't they?'

'That's been my experience,' I said. 'If we're done here, Sheriff, my boy and I better get back to work. That useless well should have been filled in three years ago. An old cow of mine—'

'Elphis.' Henry spoke like a boy in a dream. 'Her name was Elphis.'

'Elphis,' I agreed. 'She got out of the barn and decided to take a stroll on the cap, and it gave way. Didn't have the good grace to die on her own, either. I had to shoot her. Come around the back of the barn I'll show you the wages of laziness with its damn feet sticking up. We're going to bury her right where she lies, and from now on I'm going to call that old well Wilfred's Folly.'

'Well, I would, wouldn't I? It'd be somethin' to see. But I've got that bad-tempered old judge to contend with. Another time.' He hoisted himself into the car, grunting as he did so. 'Thank you for the lemonade, and for bein' so gracious. You could have been a lot less so, considering who sent me out here.'

'It's all right,' I said. 'We all have our jobs.'

'And our crosses to bear.' His sharp eyes fastened on Henry again. 'Son, Mr Lester told me you were hidin' something. He was sure of it. And you were, weren't you?'

'Yes, sir,' Henry said in his colorless and somehow awful voice. As if all his emotions had flown away, like those things in Pandora's jar when she opened it. But there was no Elphis for Henry and me; our Elphis was dead in the well.

'If he asks me, I'll tell him he was wrong,' Sheriff Jones said. 'A company lawyer don't need to know that a boy's mother put her hand to him while she was in drink.' He groped under his seat, came up with a long S-shaped tool I knew well, and held it out to Henry. 'Would you save an old man's back and shoulder, Son?'

'Yes, sir, happy to.' Henry took the crank and went around to the front of the Maxwell.

'Mind your wrist!' Jones hollered. 'She kicks like a bull!' Then he turned to me. The inquisitive glitter had gone out of his eyes. So had the green. They looked dull and gray and hard, like lakewater on a cloudy day. It was the face of a man who could beat a railroad bum within an inch of his life and never lose a minute's sleep over it. 'Mr James,' he said. 'I need to ask you something. Man to man.'

'All right,' I said. I tried to brace myself for what I felt sure was coming next: *Is there another cow in yonder well? One named Arlette?* But I was wrong.

'I can put her name and description out on the telegraph wire, if you want. She won't have gone no farther than Omaha, will she? Not on just a hundred and eighty smackers. And a woman who's spent most of her life keepin' house has no idea of how to hide out. She'll like as not be in a rooming house over on the east side, where they run cheap. I could have her brought back. *Dragged* back by the hair of the head, if you want.'

'That's a generous offer, but—'

The dull gray eyes surveyed me. 'Think it over before you say yea or nay. Sometimes a fee-male needs talking to by hand, if you take my meaning, and after that they're all right. A good whacking has a way of sweetening some gals up. Think it over.'

'I will.'

The Maxwell's engine exploded into life. I stuck out my hand – the one that had cut her throat – but Sheriff Jones didn't notice. He was busy retarding the Maxwell's spark and adjusting her throttle.

Two minutes later he was no more than a diminishing boil of dust on the farm road.

'He never even wanted to look,' Henry marveled.

'No.'

And that turned out to be a very good thing.

We had shoveled hard and fast when we saw him coming, and nothing stuck up now but one of Elphis's lower legs. The hoof was about four feet below the lip of the well. Flies circled it in a cloud. The Sheriff would have marveled, all right, and he would have marveled even more when the dirt in front of that protruding hoof began to pulse up and down.

Henry dropped his shovel and grabbed my arm. The afternoon was hot, but his hand was ice-cold. 'It's her!'

he whispered. His face seemed to be nothing but eyes. *'She's trying to get out!'*

'Stop being such a God damned ninny,' I said, but I couldn't take my eyes off that circle of heaving dirt. It was as if the well were alive, and we were seeing the beating of its hidden heart.

Then dirt and pebbles sprayed to either side and a rat surfaced. The eyes, black as beads of oil, blinked in the sunshine. It was almost as big as a full-grown cat. Caught in its whiskers was a shred of bloodstained brown burlap.

'Oh you fuck!' Henry screamed.

Something whistled inches past my ear and then the edge of Henry's shovel split the rat's head in two as it looked up into the dazzle.

'She sent it,' Henry said. He was grinning. 'The rats are hers, now.'

'No such thing. You're just upset.'

He dropped his shovel and went to the pile of rocks with which we meant to finish the job once the well was mostly filled in. There he sat down and stared at me raptly. 'Are you sure? Are you positive she ain't haunting us? People say someone who's murdered will come back to haunt whoever—'

'People say lots of things. Lightning never strikes twice in the same place, a broken mirror brings seven years' bad luck, a whippoorwill calling at midnight means someone in the family's going to die.' I sounded reasonable, but I kept looking at the dead rat. And that shred of bloodstained burlap. From her *snood*. She was still wearing it down there in the dark, only now there was a hole in it with her hair sticking up. *That look is all the rage among dead women this summer*, I thought.

'When I was a kid, I really believed that if I stepped on a crack, I'd break my mother's back,' Henry said musingly.

'There – you see?'

He brushed rock-dust from the seat of his pants, and stood beside me. 'I got him, though – I got that fucker, didn't I?'

'You did!' And because I didn't like how he sounded – no, not at all – I clapped him on the back.

Henry was still grinning. 'If the Sheriff had come back here to look, like you invited him, and seen that rat come tunneling to the top, he might have had a few more questions, don't you think?'

Something about this idea set Henry to laughing hysterically. It took him four or five minutes to laugh himself out, and he scared a murder of crows up from the fence that kept the cows out of the corn, but eventually he got past it. By the time we finished our work it was past sundown, and we could hear owls comparing notes as they launched their pre-moonrise hunts from the barn loft. The rocks on top of the vanished well were tight together, and I didn't think anymore rats would be squirming to the surface. We didn't bother replacing the broken cap; there was no need. Henry seemed almost like his normal self again, and I thought we both might get a decent night's sleep.

'What do you say to sausage, beans, and cornbread?' I asked him.

'Can I start the generator and play *Hayride Party* on the radio?'

'Yessir, you can.'

He smiled at that, his old good smile. 'Thanks, Poppa.'

I cooked enough for four farmhands, and we ate it all.

Two hours later, while I was deep in my sitting-room chair and nodding over a copy of *Silas Marner*, Henry came in from his room, dressed in just his summer under-drawers. He regarded me soberly. 'Mama always insisted on me saying my prayers, did you know that?'

I blinked at him, surprised. 'Still? No. I didn't.'

'Yes. Even after she wouldn't look at me unless I had my pants on, because she said I was too old and it wouldn't be right. But I can't pray now, or ever again. If I got down on my knees, I think God would strike me dead.'

'If there is one,' I said.

'I hope there isn't. It's lonely, but I hope there isn't. I imagine all murderers hope there isn't. Because if there's no Heaven, there's no Hell.'

'Son, I was the one who killed her.'

'No – we did it together.'

It wasn't true – he was no more than a child, and I had cozened him – but it was true to him, and I thought it always would be.

'But you don't have to worry about me, Poppa. I know you think I'll slip – probably to Shannon. Or I might get feeling guilty enough to just go into Hemingford and confess to that Sheriff.'

Of course these thoughts had crossed my mind.

Henry shook his head, slowly and emphatically. 'That Sheriff – did you see the way he looked at everything? Did you see his *eyes*?'

'Yes.'

'He'd try to put us both in the 'lectric chair, that's what I think, and never mind me not fifteen until August. He'd be there, too, lookin' at us with those hard eyes of his when they strapped us in and—'

'Stop it, Hank. That's enough.'

It wasn't, though; not for him. '—and pulled the switch. I ain't never letting that happen, if I can help it. Those eyes aren't never going to be the last thing I see.' He thought over what he'd just said. '*Ever*, I mean. *Aren't ever*.'

'Go to bed, Henry.'

'Hank.'

'Hank. Go to bed. I love you.'

He smiled. 'I know, but I don't much deserve it.' He shuffled off before I could reply.

And so to bed, as Mr Pepys says. We slept while the owls hunted and Arlette sat in her deeper darkness with the lower part of her hoof-kicked face swung off to one side. The next day the sun came up, it was a good day for corn, and we did chores.

When I came in hot and tired to fix us a noon meal, there was a covered casserole dish sitting on the porch. There was a note fluttering beneath one edge. It said: *Wilf – We are so sorry for your trouble and will help any way we can. Harlan says dont worry about paying for the harvister this summer. Please if you hear from your wife let us know. Love, Sallie Cotterie. PS: If Henry comes calling on Shan, I will send back a blueberry cake.*

I stuck the note in the front pocket of my overalls with a smile. Our life after Arlette had begun.

If God rewards us on earth for good deeds – the Old Testament suggests it's so, and the Puritans certainly believed it – then maybe Satan rewards us for evil ones. I can't say for sure, but I can say that was a good summer, with plenty of heat and sun for the corn and just enough rain to keep our acre of vegetable garden refreshed. There was thunder and lightning some afternoons, but never one of those crop-crippling winds Midwestern farmers fear. Harlan Cotterie came with his Harris Giant and it never broke down a single time. I had worried that the Farrington Company might meddle in my business, but it didn't. I got my loan from the bank with no trouble, and paid back the note in full by October, because that year corn prices were sky-high and the Great Western's freight fees were at rock bottom. If you know your history, you know that those two things – the price of produce and the price of shippage – had changed places by '23, and have stayed changed ever since. For farmers out in the middle, the Great Depression started when the Chicago Agricultural Exchange crashed the following summer. But the summer of 1922 was as perfect as any farmer could hope for. Only one incident marred it, having to do with another of our bovine goddesses, and that I will tell you about soon.

Mr Lester came out twice. He tried to badger us, but he had nothing to badger with, and he must have known it, because he was looking pretty harried that July. I imagine his bosses were badgering *him*, and he was only passing it along. Or trying to. The first time, he asked a lot of questions that really weren't questions at all, but insinuations. Did I think my wife had had an accident? She must have, didn't I think, or she would either have contacted him in order to make a cash settlement on those 100 acres or just crept back to the farm with her (metaphorical) tail between her legs. Or did I think she had fallen afoul of some bad actor while on the road? Such things did happen, didn't they, from time to time? And it would certainly be convenient for me, wouldn't it?

The second time he showed up, he looked desperate as well as harried, and came right out with it: had my wife had an accident right there on the farm? Was that what had happened? Was it why she hadn't turned up either alive or dead?

'Mr Lester, if you're asking me if I murdered my wife, the answer is no.'

'Well of course you'd say so, wouldn't you?'

'That's your last question to me, sir. Get in yonder truck, drive away, and don't come back here. If you do, I'll take an axe-handle to you.'

'You'd go to jail for assault!' He was wearing a celluloid collar that day, and it had come all askew. It was almost possible to feel sorry for him as he stood there with that collar poking into the underside of his chin and sweat cutting lines through the dust on his chubby face, his lips twitching and his eyes bulging.

'No such thing. I have warned you off my property, as is my right, and I intend to send a registered letter to your firm stating that very thing. Come back again and that's trespassing and I *will* beat you. Take warning, sir.' Lars Olsen, who had brought Lester out again in his Red Baby, had all but cupped his hands around his ears to hear better.

When Lester reached the doorless passenger side of the truck, he whirled with an arm outstretched and a finger pointing, like a courtroom lawyer with a bent for the theatrical. 'I think you killed her! And sooner or later, murder will out!'

Henry – or Hank, as he now preferred to be called – came out of the barn. He had been pitching hay and he held the pitchfork across his chest like a rifle at port arms. 'What *I* think is you better get out of here before you start bleeding,' he said. The kind and rather timid boy I had known until the summer of '22 would never have said such a thing, but this one did, and Lester saw that he meant it. He got in. With no door to slam, he settled for crossing his arms over his chest.

'Come back anytime, Lars,' I said pleasantly, 'but don't bring him, no matter how much he offers you to cart his useless ass.'

'No, sir, Mr James,' Lars said, and off they went.

I turned to Henry. 'Would you have stuck him with that pitchfork?'

'Yessir. Made him squeal.' Then, unsmiling, he went back into the barn.

But he wasn't *always* unsmiling that summer, and Shannon Cotterie was the reason why. He saw a lot of her (more of her than was good for either of them; that I found out in the fall). She began coming to the house on Tuesday and Thursday afternoons, long-skirted and neatly bonneted, toting a side-sack loaded with good things to eat. She said she knew 'what men cook' – as though she were 30 instead of just 15 – and said she intended to see we had at least two decent suppers a week. And although I had only one of her mother's casseroles for comparison, I'd have to say that even at 15 she was the superior cook. Henry and I just threw steaks in a skillet on the stove; she had a way of seasoning that made plain old chew-meat delicious. She brought fresh vegetables in her side-sack – not just carrots and peas but exotic (to us) things like asparagus and fat green beans she cooked with pearl onions and bacon. There was even dessert. I can close my eyes in this shabby hotel room and smell her pastry. I can see her standing at the kitchen counter with her bottom swaying as she beat eggs or whipped cream.

Generous was the word for Shannon: of hip, of bust, of heart. She was gentle with Henry, and she cared for him. That made me care for her . . . only that's too thin, Reader. I loved her, and we both loved Henry. After those Tuesday and Thursday dinners, I'd insist on doing the washing-up and send them out on the porch. Sometimes I heard them murmuring to each other, and would peek out to see them sitting side by side in the wicker chairs, looking out at West Field and holding hands like an old married couple. Other times I spied them kissing, and there was nothing of the old married couple about that at all. There was a sweet urgency to those kisses that belongs only to the very young, and I stole away with my heart aching.

One hot Tuesday afternoon she came early. Her father was out in our North Field on his harvester, Henry riding with him, a little crew of Indians from the Shoshone reservation in Lyme Biska walking along behind . . . and behind them, Old Pie driving the gather-truck. Shannon asked for a dipper of cold water, which I was glad to provide. She stood there on the shady side of the house, looking impossibly cool in a voluminous dress that covered her from throat to shin and shoulder to wrist – a Quaker dress, almost. Her manner was grave, perhaps even scared, and for a moment I was scared myself. *He's told her*, I thought. That turned out not to be true. Except, in a way, it was.

'Mr James, is Henry sick?'

'Sick? Why, no. Healthy as a horse, I'd say. And eats like one, too. You've seen that for yourself. Although I think even a man who *was* sick would have trouble saying no to your cooking, Shannon.'

That earned me a smile, but it was of the distracted variety. 'He's different this summer. I always used to know what he was thinking, but now I don't. He *broods*.'

'Does he?' I asked (too heartily).

'You haven't seen it?'

'No, ma'am.' (I had.) 'He seems like his old self to me. But he cares for you an awful lot, Shan. Maybe what looks like brooding to you feels like the lovesicks to him.'

I thought that would get me a real smile, but no. She touched my wrist. Her hand was cool from the dipper handle. 'I've thought of that, but . . .' The rest she blurted out. 'Mr James, if he was sweet on someone else – one of the girls from school – you'd tell me, wouldn't you? You wouldn't try to . . . to spare my feelings?'

I laughed at that, and I could see her pretty face lighten with relief. 'Shan, listen to me. Because I *am* your friend. Summer's always a hardworking time, and with Arlette gone, Hank and I have been busier than one-armed paperhangers. When we come in at night, we eat a meal – a fine one, if you happen to show up – and then read for an hour. Sometimes he talks about how he misses his mama. After that we go to bed, and the next day we get up and do it all again. He barely has time to spark *you*, let alone another girl.'

'He's sparked me, all right,' she said, and looked off to where her father's harvester was chugging along the skyline.

'Well . . . that's good, isn't it?'

'I just thought . . . he's so quiet now . . . so moody . . . sometimes he looks off into the distance and I have to say his name twice or three times before he hears me and answers.' She blushed fiercely. 'Even his kisses seem different. I don't know how to explain it, but they do. And if you ever tell him I said that, I'll die. I will just *die*.'

'I never would,' I said. 'Friends don't peach on friends.'

'I guess I'm being a silly-billy. And of course he misses his mama, I know he does. But so many of the girls at school are prettier than me . . . prettier than me . . .'

I tilted her chin up so she was looking at me. 'Shannon Cotterie, when my boy looks at you, he sees the prettiest girl in the world. And he's right. Why, if I was his age, I'd spark you myself.'

'Thank you,' she said. Tears like tiny diamonds stood in the corners of her eyes.

'The only thing you need to worry about is putting him back in his place if he gets out of it. Boys can get pretty steamed up, you know. And if I'm out of line, you just go on and tell me so. That's another thing that's all right, if it's between friends.'

She hugged me then, and I hugged her back. A good strong hug, but perhaps better for Shannon than me. Because Arlette was between us. She was between me and everyone else in the summer of 1922, and it was the same for Henry. Shannon had just told me so.

*   *   *

One night in August, with the good picking done and Old Pie's crew paid up and back on the rez, I woke to the sound of a cow lowing. *I overslept milking time*, I thought, but when I fumbled my father's pocket watch off the table beside my bed and peered at it, I saw it was quarter past three in the morning. I put the watch to my ear to see if it was still ticking, but a look out the window into the moonless dark would have served the same purpose. Those weren't the mildly uncomfortable calls of a cow needing to be rid of her milk, either. It was the sound of an animal in pain. Cows sometimes sound that way when they're calving, but our goddesses were long past that stage of their lives.

I got up, started out the door, then went back to the closet for my .22. I heard Henry sawing wood behind the closed door of his room as I hurried past with the rifle in one hand and my boots in the other. I hoped he wouldn't wake up and want to join me on what could be a dangerous errand. There were only a few wolves left on the plains by then, but Old Pie had told me there was summer-sick in some of the foxes along the Platte and Medicine Creek. It was what the Shoshone called rabies, and a rabid critter in the barn was the most likely cause of those cries.

Once I was outside the house, the agonized lowing was very loud, and hollow, somehow. Echoing. *Like a cow in a well*, I thought. That thought chilled the flesh on my arms and made me grip the .22 tighter.

By the time I reached the barn doors and shouldered the right one open, I could hear the rest of the cows starting to moo in sympathy, but those cries were calm inquiries compared to the agonized bawling that had awakened me . . . and would awaken Henry, too, if I didn't put an end to what was causing it. There was a carbon arc-lamp hanging on a hook to the right of the door – we didn't use an open flame in the barn unless we absolutely had to, especially in the summertime, when the loft was loaded with hay and every corncrib crammed full to the top.

I felt for the spark-button and pushed it. A brilliant circle of blue-white radiance leaped out. At first my eyes were too dazzled to make out anything; I could only hear those painful cries and the hoof-thuds as one of our goddesses tried to escape from whatever was hurting her. It was Achelois. When my eyes adjusted a bit, I saw her tossing her head from side to side, backing up until her hindquarters hit the door of her stall – third on the right, as you walked up the aisle – and then lurching forward again. The other cows were working themselves into a full-bore panic.

I hauled on my muckies, then trotted to the stall with the .22 tucked under my left arm. I threw the door open, and stepped back. Achelois means 'she who drives away pain,' but this Achelois was in agony. When she blundered into the aisle, I saw her back legs were smeared with blood. She reared up like a horse (something I never saw a cow do before), and when she did, I saw a huge Norway rat clinging to one of her teats. The weight had stretched the pink stub to a taut length of cartilage. Frozen in surprise (and horror), I thought of how, as a child, Henry would sometimes pull a string of pink bubble-gum out of his mouth. *Don't do that*, Arlette would scold him. *No one wants to look at what you've been chewing.*

I raised the gun, then lowered it. How could I shoot, with the rat swinging back and forth like a living weight at the end of a pendulum?

In the aisle now, Achelois lowed and shook her head from side to side, as if that might somehow help. Once all four of her feet were back on the floor, the rat was able to stand on the hay-littered barnboards. It was like some strange freak puppy with beads of bloodstained milk in its whiskers. I looked around for something to hit it with, but before I could grab the broom Henry had left leaning against Phemonoe's stall, Achelois reared again and the rat thumped to the floor. At first I thought she had simply dislodged it, but then I saw the pink and wrinkled stub protruding from the rat's mouth, like a flesh cigar. The damned thing had torn one of poor Achelois's teats right off. She laid her head against one of the barn beams and mooed at me tiredly, as if to say: *I've given you milk all these years and offered no trouble, not like some I could mention, so why did you let this happen to me?* Blood was pooling beneath her udder. Even in my shock and revulsion, I didn't think she would die of her wound, but the sight of her — and of the rat, with her blameless teat in its mouth — filled me with rage.

I still didn't shoot at it, partly because I was afraid of fire, but mostly because, with the carbon lamp in one hand, I was afraid I'd miss. Instead, I brought the rifle-stock down, hoping to kill this intruder as Henry had killed the survivor from the well with his shovel. But Henry was a boy with quick reflexes, and I was a man of middle age who had been roused from a sound sleep. The rat avoided me with ease and went trotting up the center aisle. The severed teat bobbed up and down in its mouth, and I realized the rat was eating it — warm and no doubt still full of milk — even as it ran. I gave chase, smacked at it twice more, and missed both times. Then I saw where it was running: the pipe leading into the defunct livestock well. Of course! Rat Boulevard! With the well filled in, it was their only means of egress. Without it, they'd have been buried alive. Buried with *her.*

But surely, I thought, *that thing is too big for the pipe. It must have come from outside — a nest in the manure pile, perhaps.*

It leaped for the opening, and as it did so, it elongated

its body in the most amazing fashion. I swung the stock of the varmint gun one last time and shattered it on the lip of the pipe. The rat I missed entirely. When I lowered the carbon lamp to the pipe's mouth, I caught one blurred glimpse of its hairless tail slithering away into the darkness, and heard its little claws scraping on the galvanized metal. Then it was gone. My heart was pounding hard enough to put white dots in front of my eyes. I drew in a deep breath, but with it came a stench of putrefaction and decay so strong that I fell back with my hand over my nose. The need to scream was strangled by the need to retch. With that smell in my nostrils I could almost see Arlette at the other end of the pipe, her flesh now teeming with bugs and maggots, liquefying; her face beginning to drip off her skull, the grin of her lips giving way to the longer-lasting bone grin that lay beneath.

I crawled back from that awful pipe on all fours, spraying vomit first to my left and then to my right, and when my supper was all gone, I gagged up long strings of bile. Through watering eyes I saw that Achelois had gone back into her stall. That was good. At least I wasn't going to have to chase her through the corn and put a nose-halter on her to lead her back.

What I wanted to do first was plug the pipe – I wanted to do that before anything – but as my gorge quieted, clear thinking reasserted itself. Achelois was the priority. She was a good milker. More important, she was my responsibility. I kept a medicine chest in the little barn office where I did the books. In the chest I found a large can of Rawleigh Antiseptic Salve. There was a pile of clean rags in the corner. I took half of them and went back to Achelois's stall. I closed the door of her stall to minimize the risk of being kicked, and sat on the milking stool. I think part of me felt I *deserved* to be kicked. But dear old Achelois stilled when I stroked her flank and whispered, 'Soo, Boss, soo, Bossy-boss,' and although she shivered when I smeared the salve on her hurt part, she stood quiet.

When I'd taken what steps I could to prevent infection, I used the rags to wipe up my vomit. It was important to do a good job, for any farmer will tell you that human vomit attracts predators every bit as much as a garbage-hole that hasn't been adequately covered. Raccoons and woodchucks, of course, but mostly rats. Rats love human leavings.

I had a few rags left over, but they were Arlette's kitchen castoffs and too thin for my next job. I took the hand-scythe from its peg, lit my way to our woodpile, and chopped a ragged square from the heavy canvas that covered it. Back in the barn, I bent down and held the lamp close to the pipe's mouth, wanting to make sure the rat (or another; where there was one, there would surely be more) wasn't lurking, ready to defend its territory, but it was empty for as far as I could see, which was four feet or so. There were no droppings, and that didn't surprise me. It was an active thoroughfare — now their *only* thoroughfare — and they wouldn't foul it as long as they could do their business outside.

I stuffed the canvas into the pipe. It was stiff and bulky, and in the end I had to use a broomhandle to poke it all the way in, but I managed. 'There,' I said. 'See how you like that. Choke on it.'

I went back and looked at Achelois. She stood quietly, and gave me a mild look over her shoulder as I stroked her. I knew then and know now she was only a cow — farmers hold few romantic notions about the natural world, you'll find — but that look still brought tears to my eyes, and I had to stifle a sob. *I know you did your best*, it said. *I know it's not your fault.*

But it was.

I could hear Henry snoring. I thought I would lie awake long, and when I went to sleep I would dream of the rat scurrying up the hay-littered barnboards toward its escape-hatch with that teat in its mouth, but I fell asleep at once and my sleep was both dreamless and restorative. I woke with morning light flooding the room and the stench of my dead wife's decaying body thick on my hands, sheets, and pillow-case. I sat bolt upright, gasping but already aware that the smell was an illusion. That smell was my bad dream. I had it not at night but by the morning's first, sanest light, and with my eyes wide open.

I expected infection from the rat-bite in spite of the salve, but there was none. Achelois died later that year, but not of that. She never gave milk again, however; not a single drop. I should have butchered her, but I didn't have the heart to do it. She had suffered too much on my account.

The next day, I handed Henry a list of supplies and told him to take the truck over to The Home and get them. A great, dazzled smile broke across his face.

'The truck? *Me?* On my own?'

'You still know all the forward gears? And you can still find reverse?'

'Gosh, sure!'

'Then I think you're ready. Maybe not for Omaha just yet – or even Lincoln – but if you take her slow, you ought to be just fine in Hemingford Home.'

'Thanks!' He threw his arms around me and kissed my cheek. For a moment it seemed like we were friends again. I even let myself believe it a little, although in my heart I knew better. The evidence might be belowground, but the truth was between us, and always would be.

I gave him a leather wallet with money in it. 'That was your grandfather's. You might as well keep it; I was going to give it to you for your birthday this fall, anyway. There's money inside. You can keep what's left over, if there is any.' I almost added, *And don't bring back any stray dogs*, but stopped myself in time. That had been his mother's stock witticism.

He tried to thank me again, and couldn't. It was all too much.

'Stop by Lars Olsen's smithy on your way back and fuel up. Mind me, now, or you'll be on foot instead of behind the wheel when you get home.'

'I won't forget. And Poppa?'

'Yes.'

He shuffled his feet, then looked at me shyly. 'Could I stop at Cotteries' and ask Shan to come?'

'No,' I said, and his face fell before I added: 'You ask Sallie or Harlan if Shan can come. And you make sure you tell them that you've never driven in town before. I'm putting you on your honor, Son.'

As if either of us had any left.

I watched by the gate until our old truck disappeared into a ball of its own dust. There was a lump in my throat that I couldn't swallow. I had a stupid but very strong premonition that I would never see him again. I suppose it's something most parents feel the first time they see a child going away on his own and face the realization that if a child is old enough to be sent on errands without supervision, he's not totally a child any longer. But I couldn't spend too much time wallowing in my feelings; I had an important chore to do, and I'd sent Henry away so I could attend to it by myself. He would see what had happened to the cow, of course, and probably guess what had done it, but I thought I could still ease the knowledge for him a little.

I first checked on Achelois, who seemed listless but

otherwise fine. Then I checked the pipe. It was still plugged, but I was under no illusions; it might take time, but eventually the rats would gnaw through the canvas. I had to do better. I took a bag of Portland cement around to the house-well and mixed up a batch in an old pail. Back in the barn, while I waited for it to thicken, I poked the swatch of canvas even deeper into the pipe. I got it in at least two feet, and those last two feet I packed with cement. By the time Henry got back (and in fine spirits; he had indeed taken Shannon, and they had shared an icecream soda bought with change from the errands), it had hardened. I suppose a few of the rats must have been out foraging, but I had no doubt I'd immured most of them – including the one that had savaged poor Achelois – down there in the dark. And down there in the dark they would die. If not of suffocation, then of starvation once their unspeakable pantry was exhausted.

So I thought then.

In the years between 1916 and 1922, even stupid Nebraska farmers prospered. Harlan Cotterie, being far from stupid, prospered more than most. His farm showed it. He added a barn and a silo in 1919, and in 1920 he put in a deep well that pumped an unbelievable six gallons per minute. A year later, he added indoor plumbing (although he sensibly kept the backyard privy). Then, three times a week, he and his womenfolk could enjoy what was an unbelievable luxury that far out in the country: hot baths and showers supplied not by pots of water heated on the kitchen stove but from pipes that first brought the water from the well and then carried it away to the sump. It was the showerbath that revealed the secret Shannon Cotterie had been keeping, although I suppose I already knew, and had since the day she said, *He's sparked me, all right* – speaking in a flat, lusterless voice that was unlike her, and looking not at me but off at the silhouettes of her father's harvester and the gleaners trudging behind it.

This was near the end of September, with the corn all picked for another year but plenty of garden-harvesting left to do. One Saturday afternoon, while Shannon was enjoying the showerbath, her mother came along the back hall with a load of laundry she'd taken in from the line early, because it was looking like rain. Shannon probably thought she had closed the bathroom door all the way – most ladies are private about their bathroom duties, and Shannon Cotterie had a special reason to feel that way as the summer of 1922 gave way to fall – but perhaps it came off the latch and swung open partway. Her mother happened to glance in, and although the old sheet that served as a shower-curtain was pulled all the way around on its U-shaped rail, the spray had rendered it translucent. There was no need for Sallie to see the girl herself; she saw the *shape* of the girl, for once without one of her voluminous Quaker-style dresses to hide. That was all it took. The girl was five months along, or near to it; she probably could not have kept her secret much longer in any case.

Two days later, Henry came home from school (he now took the truck) looking frightened and guilty. 'Shan hasn't been there the last two days,' he said, 'so I stopped by Cotteries' to ask if she was all right. I thought she might have come down with the Spanish Flu. They wouldn't let me in. Mrs Cotterie just told me to get on, and said her husband would come to talk to you tonight, after his chores were done. I ast if I could do anything, and she said, "You've done enough, Henry."'

Then I remembered what Shan had said. Henry put his face in his hands and said, 'She's pregnant, Poppa, and they found out. I know that's it. We want to get married, but I'm afraid they won't let us.'

'Never mind them,' I said, '*I* won't let you.'

He looked at me from wounded, streaming eyes. 'Why not?'

I thought: *You saw what it came to between your mother and me and you even have to ask?* But what I said was, 'She's 15 years old, and you won't even be that for another two weeks.'

'But we love each other!'

O, that loonlike cry. That milksop hoot. My hands were clenched on the legs of my overalls, and I had to force them open and flat. Getting angry would serve no purpose. A boy needed a mother to discuss a thing like this with, but his was sitting at the bottom of a filled-in well, no doubt attended by a retinue of dead rats.

'I know you do, Henry—'

'*Hank!* And others get married that young!'

Once they had; not so much since the century turned and the frontiers closed. But this I didn't say. What I said was that I had no money to give them a start. Maybe by '25, if crops and prices stayed good, but now there was nothing. And with a baby on the way—

'There *would* be enough!' he said. 'If you hadn't been such a bugger about that hundred acres, there'd be *plenty*! S*he* would've given me some of it! And *she* wouldn't have talked to me this way!'

At first I was too shocked to say anything. It had been six weeks or more since Arlette's name – or even the vague pronounal alias *she* – had passed between us.

He was looking at me defiantly. And then, far down our stub of road, I saw Harlan Cotterie on his way. I had always considered him my friend, but a daughter who turns up pregnant has a way of changing such things.

'No, she wouldn't have talked to you this way,' I agreed, and made myself look him straight in the eye. 'She would have talked to you worse. And laughed, likely as not. If you search your heart, Son, you'll know it.'

'No!'

'Your mother called Shannon a little baggage, and then told you to keep your willy in your pants. It was her last advice, and although it was as crude and hurtful as most of what she had to say, you should have followed it.'

Henry's anger collapsed. 'It was only after that . . . after that night . . . that we . . . Shan didn't want to, but I talked her into it. And once we started, she liked it as much as I did. Once we started, she asked for it.' He said that with a strange, half-sick pride, then shook his head wearily. 'Now that hundred acres just sits there sprouting weeds, and I'm in Dutch. If Momma was here, she'd help me fix it. Money fixes everything, that's what *he* says.' Henry nodded at the approaching ball of dust.

'If you don't remember how tight your momma was with a dollar, then you forget too fast for your own good,' I said. 'And if you've forgotten how she slapped you across the mouth that time—'

'I ain't,' he said sullenly. Then, more sullenly still: 'I thought you'd help me.'

'I mean to try. Right now I want you to make yourself scarce. You being here when Shannon's father turns up would be like waving a red rag in front of a bull. Let me see where we are — and how he is — and I may call you out on the porch.' I took his wrist. 'I'm going to do my best for you, Son.'

He pulled his wrist out of my grasp. 'You better.'

He went into the house, and just before Harlan pulled up in his new car (a Nash as green and gleaming under its coating of dust as a bottlefly's back), I heard the screen door slam out back.

The Nash chugged, backfired, and died. Harlan got out, took off his duster, folded it, and laid it on the seat. He'd worn the duster because he was dressed for the occasion: white shirt, string tie, good Sunday pants held

up by a belt with a silver buckle. He hitched at that,
getting the pants set the way he wanted them just below
his tidy little paunch. He'd always been good to me, and
I'd always considered us not just friends but good friends,
yet in that moment I hated him. Not because he'd come
to tax me about my son; God knows I would have done
the same, if our positions had been reversed. No, it
was the brand-new shiny green Nash. It was the silver
belt buckle made in the shape of a dolphin. It was the
new silo, painted bright red, and the indoor plumbing.
Most of all it was the plain-faced, biddable wife he'd left
back at his farm, no doubt making supper in spite of her
worry. The wife whose sweetly given reply in the face of
any problem would be, *Whatever you think is best, dear.*
Women, take note: a wife like that never needs to fear
bubbling away the last of her life through a cut throat.

He strode to the porch steps. I stood and held out
my hand, waiting to see if he'd take it or leave it. There
was a hesitation while he considered the pros and cons,
but in the end he gave it a brief squeeze before letting
loose. 'We've got a considerable problem here, Wilf,' he said.

'I know it. Henry just told me. Better late than never.'

'Better never at all,' he said grimly.

'Will you sit down?'

He considered this, too, before taking what had always
been Arlette's rocker. I knew he didn't want to sit – a
man who's mad and upset doesn't feel good about sitting
– but he did, just the same.

'Would you want some iced tea? There's no lemonade,
Arlette was the lemonade expert, but—'

He waved me quiet with one pudgy hand. Pudgy but
hard. Harlan was one of the richest farmers in Hemingford
County, but he was no straw boss; when it came to haying
or harvest, he was right out there with the hired help. 'I
want to get back before sundown. I don't see worth a shit

by those headlamps. My girl has got a bun in her oven, and I guess you know who did the damn cooking.'

'Would it help to say I'm sorry?'

'No.' His lips were pressed tight together, and I could see hot blood beating on both sides of his neck. 'I'm madder than a hornet, and what makes it worse is that I've got no one to be mad *at*. I can't be mad at the kids because they're just kids, although if she wasn't with child, I'd turn Shannon over my knee and paddle her for not doing better when she *knew* better. She was raised better and churched better, too.'

I wanted to ask him if he was saying Henry was raised wrong. I kept my mouth shut instead, and let him say all the things he'd been fuming about on his drive over here. He'd thought up a speech, and once he said it, he might be easier to deal with.

'I'd like to blame Sallie for not seeing the girl's condition sooner, but first-timers usually carry high, everyone knows that . . . and my God, you know the sort of dresses Shan wears. That's not a new thing, either. She's been wearing those granny-go-to-meetin' dresses since she was 12 and started getting her . . .'

He held his pudgy hands out in front of his chest. I nodded.

'And I'd like to blame *you*, because it seems like you skipped that talk fathers usually have with sons.' *As if you'd know anything about raising sons*, I thought. 'The one about how he's got a pistol in his pants and he should keep the safety on.' A sob caught in his throat and he cried, 'My . . . little . . . *girl* . . . is too young to be a mother!'

Of course there was blame for me Harlan didn't know about. If I hadn't put Henry in a situation where he was desperate for a woman's love, Shannon might not be in the fix she was in. I also could have asked if Harlan had maybe saved a little blame for himself while he was busy sharing it out. But I held quiet. Quiet never came naturally to me, but living with Arlette had given me plenty of practice.

'Only I can't blame you, either, because your wife went and run off this spring, and it's natural your attention would lapse at a time like that. So I went out back and chopped damn near half a cord of wood before I came over here, trying to get some of that mad out, and it must have worked. I shook your hand, didn't I?'

The self-congratulation I heard in his voice made me itch to say, *Unless it was rape, I think it still takes two to tango.* But I just said, 'Yes, you did,' and left it at that.

'Well, that brings us to what you're going to do about it. You and that boy who sat at my table and ate the food my wife cooked for him.'

Some devil – the creature that comes into a fellow, I suppose, when the Conniving Man leaves – made me say, 'Henry wants to marry her and give the baby a name.'

'That's so God damned ridiculous I don't want to hear it. I won't say Henry doesn't have a pot to piss in nor a window to throw it out of – I know you've done right, Wilf, or as right as you can, but that's the best I can say. These have been fat years, and you're still only one step ahead of the bank. Where are you going to be when the years get lean again? And they always do. If you had the cash from that back hundred, then it might be different – cash cushions hard times, everyone knows that – but with Arlette gone, there they sit, like a constipated old maid on a chamberpot.'

For just a moment part of me tried to consider how things would have been if I had given in to Arlette about that fucking land, as I had about so many other things. *I'd be living in stink, that's how it would have been. I would have had to dig out the old spring for the cows, because cows won't drink from a brook that's got blood and pigs' guts floating in it.*

True. But I'd be living instead of just existing, Arlette would be living with me, and Henry wouldn't be the sullen, anguished, difficult boy he had turned into. The boy who had gotten his friend since childhood into a peck of trouble.

'Well, what do you want to do?' I asked. 'I doubt you made this trip with nothing in mind.'

He appeared not to have heard me. He was looking out across the fields to where his new silo stood on the horizon. His face was heavy and sad, but I've come too far and written too much to lie; that expression did not move me much. 1922 had been the worst year of my life, one where I'd turned into a man I no longer knew, and Harlan Cotterie was just another washout on a rocky and miserable stretch of road.

'She's bright,' Harlan said. 'Mrs McReady at school says Shan's the brightest pupil she's taught in her whole career, and that stretches back almost 40 years. She's good in English, and she's even better in the maths, which Mrs McReady says is rare in girls. She can do triggeronomy, Wilf. Did you know that? Mrs McReady herself can't do triggeronomy.'

No, I hadn't known, but I knew how to say the word. I felt, however, that this might not be the time to correct my neighbor's pronunciation.

'Sallie wanted to send her to the normal school in Omaha. They've taken girls as well as boys since 1918, although no females have graduated so far.' He gave me a look that was hard to take: mingled disgust and hostility. 'The females always want to get *married*, you see. And *have babies*. Join Eastern *Star* and sweep the God damned *floor.*'

He sighed.

'Shan could be the first. She has the skills and she has the brains. You didn't know that, did you?'

No, in truth I had not. I had simply made an assumption – one of many that I now know to have been wrong – that she was farm wife material, and no more.

'She might even teach college. We planned to send her to that school as soon as she turned 17.'

Sallie planned, is what you mean, I thought. *Left to your own devices, such a crazy idea never would have crossed your farmer's mind.*

'Shan was willing, and the money was put aside. It was all arranged.' He turned to look at me, and I heard the tendons in his neck creak. 'It's *still* all arranged. But first – almost right away – she's going to the St Eusebia Catholic Home for Girls in Omaha. She doesn't know it yet, but it's going to happen. Sallie talked about sending her to Deland – Sal's sister lives there – or to my aunt and uncle in Lyme Biska, but I don't trust any of those people to carry through on what we've decided. Nor does a girl who causes this kind of problem deserve to go to people she knows and loves.'

'What is it you've decided, Harl? Besides sending your daughter to some kind of an . . . I don't know . . . orphanage?'

He bristled. 'It's not an orphanage. It's a clean, wholesome, and busy place. So I've been told. I've been on the exchange, and all the reports I get are good ones. She'll have chores, she'll have her schooling, and in another four months she'll have her baby. When that's done, the kid will be given up for adoption. The sisters at St Eusebia will see to that. Then she can come home, and in another year and a half she can go to teachers' college, just like Sallie wants. And me, of course. Sallie and me.'

'What's my part in this? I assume I must have one.'

'Are you smarting on me, Wilf? I know you've had a tough year, but I still won't bear you smarting on me.'

'I'm not smarting on you, but you need to know

you're not the only one who's mad and ashamed. Just tell me what you want, and maybe we can stay friends.'

The singularly cold little smile with which he greeted this — just a twitch of the lips and a momentary appearance of dimples at the corners of his mouth — said a great deal about how little hope he held out for *that*.

'I know you're not rich, but you still need to step up and take your share of the responsibility. Her time at the home — the sisters call it pre-natal care — is going to cost me 300 dollars. Sister Camilla called it a donation when I talked to her on the phone, but I know a fee when I hear one.'

'If you're going to ask me to split it with you—'

'I know you can't lay your hands on 150 dollars, but you better be able to lay them on 75, because that's what the tutor's going to cost. The one who's going to help her keep up with her lessons.'

'I can't do that. Arlette cleaned me out when she left.' But for the first time I found myself wondering if she might've socked a little something away. That business about the 200 she was supposed to have taken when she ran off had been a pure lie, but even pin-and-ribbon money would help in this situation. I made a mental note to check the cupboards and the canisters in the kitchen.

'Take another shortie loan from the bank,' he said. 'You paid the last one back, I hear.'

Of course he heard. Such things are supposed to be private, but men like Harlan Cotterie have long ears. I felt a fresh wave of dislike for him. He had loaned me the use of his corn harvester and only taken 20 dollars for the use of it? So what? He was asking for that and more, as though his precious daughter had never spread her legs and said *come on in and paint the walls*.

'I had crop money to pay it back with,' I said. 'Now

I don't. I've got my land and my house and that's pretty much it.'

'You find a way,' he said. 'Mortgage the house, if that's what it takes. 75 dollars is your share, and compared to having your boy changing didies at the age of 15, I think you're getting off cheap.'

He stood up. I did, too. 'And if I can't find a way? What then, Harl? You send the Sheriff?'

His lips curled in an expression of contempt that turned my dislike of him to hate. It happened in an instant, and I still feel that hate today, when so many other feelings have been burned out of my heart. 'I'd never go to law on a thing like this. But if you don't take your share of the responsibility, you and me's done.' He squinted into the declining daylight. 'I'm going. Got to, if I want to get back before dark. I won't need the 75 for a couple of weeks, so you got that long. And I won't come dunning you for it. If you don't, you don't. Just don't say you can't, because I know better. You should have let her sell that acreage to Farrington, Wilf. If you'd done that, she'd still be here and you'd have some money in hand. And my daughter might not be in the fam'ly way.'

In my mind, I pushed him off the porch and jumped on his hard round belly with both feet when he tried to get up. Then I got my hand-scythe out of the barn and put it through one of his eyes. In reality, I stood with one hand on the railing and watched him trudge down the steps.

'Do you want to talk to Henry?' I asked. 'I can call him. He feels as bad about this as I do.'

Harlan didn't break stride. 'She was clean and your boy filthied her up. If you hauled him out here, I might knock him down. I might not be able to help myself.'

I wondered about that. Henry was getting his growth,

he was strong, and perhaps most important of all, he knew about murder. Harl Cotterie didn't.

He didn't need to crank the Nash but only push a button. Being prosperous was nice in all sorts of ways. '75 is what I need to close this business,' he called over the punch and blat of the engine. Then he whirled around the chopping block, sending George and his retinue flying, and headed back to his farm with its big generator and indoor plumbing.

When I turned around, Henry was standing beside me, looking sallow and furious. 'They can't send her away like that.'

So he had been listening. I can't say I was surprised.

'Can and will,' I said. 'And if you try something stupid and headstrong, you'll only make a bad situation worse.'

'We could run away. We wouldn't get caught. If we could get away with . . . with what we did . . . then I guess I could get away with eloping off to Colorado with my gal.'

'You couldn't,' I said, 'because you'd have no money. Money fixes everything, he says. Well, this is what I say: *no* money *spoils* everything. I know it, and Shannon will, too. She's got her baby to watch out for now—'

'Not if they make her give it away!'

'That doesn't change how a woman feels when she's got the chap in her belly. A chap makes them wise in ways men don't understand. I haven't lost any respect for you or her just because she's going to have a baby – you two aren't the first, and you won't be the last, even if Mr High and Mighty had the idea she was only going to use what's between her legs in the water-closet. But if you asked a five-months-pregnant girl to run off with you . . . and she agreed . . . I'd lose respect for both of you.'

'What do you know?' he asked with infinite contempt. 'You couldn't even cut a throat without making a mess of it.'

I was speechless. He saw it, and left me that way.

He went off to school the next day without any argument even though his sweetie was no longer there. Probably because I let him take the truck. A boy will take any excuse to drive a truck when driving's new. But of course the new wears off. The new wears off everything, and it usually doesn't take long. What's beneath is gray and shabby, more often than not. Like a rat's hide.

Once he was gone, I went into the kitchen. I poured the sugar, flour, and salt out of their tin canisters and stirred through them. There was nothing. I went into the bedroom and searched her clothes. There was nothing. I looked in her shoes and there was nothing. But each time I found nothing, I became more sure there was *something*.

I had chores in the garden, but instead of doing them, I went out back of the barn to where the old well had been. Weeds were growing on it now: witchgrass and scraggly fall goldenrod. Elphis was down there, and Arlette was, too. Arlette with her face cocked to the side. Arlette with her clown's grin. Arlette in her *snood*.

'Where is it, you contrary bitch?' I asked her. 'Where did you hide it?'

I tried to empty my mind, which was what my father advised me to do when I'd misplaced a tool or one of my few precious books. After a little while I went back into the house, back into the bedroom, back into the closet. There were two hatboxes on the top shelf. In the first one I found nothing but a hat – the white one she wore to church (when she could trouble herself to go, which was about once a month). The hat in the other box was red, and I'd never seen her wear it. It looked like a whore's hat to me. Tucked into the satin inner band, folded into tiny squares no bigger than pills, were two 20-dollar bills. I tell you now, sitting here in this cheap hotel room and listening to the rats scuttering and scampering in the walls (yes, my old friends are here), that those two 20-dollar bills were the seal on my damnation.

Because they weren't enough. You see that, don't you? Of course you do. One doesn't need to be an expert in triggeronomy to know that one needs to add 35 to 40 to make 75. Doesn't sound like much, does it? But in those days you could buy two months' worth of groceries for 35 dollars, or a good used harness at Lars Olsen's smithy. You could buy a train ticket all the way to Sacramento . . . which I sometimes wish I had done.

35.

And sometimes when I lie in bed at night, I can actually *see* that number. It flashes red, like a warning not to cross a road because a train is coming. I tried to cross anyway, and the train ran me down. If each of us has a Conniving Man inside, each of us also has a Lunatic. And on those nights when I can't sleep because the flashing number won't *let* me sleep, my Lunatic says it was a conspiracy: that Cotterie, Stoppenhauser, and the Farrington shyster were all in it together. I know better, of course (at least in daylight). Cotterie and Mr Attorney Lester might have had a talk with Stoppenhauser later on – after I did what I did – but it was surely innocent to begin with; Stoppenhauser was actually trying to help me out . . . and do a little business for Home Bank & Trust, of course. But when Harlan or Lester – or both of them together – saw an opportunity, they took it. The Conniving Man outconnived: how do you like that? By then I hardly cared, because by then I had lost my son, but do you know who I really blame?

Arlette.

Yes.

Because it was she who left those two bills inside her red whore's hat for me to find. And do you see how fiendishly clever she was? Because it wasn't the *40* that did me in; it was the money between that and what Cotterie demanded for his pregnant daughter's tutor; what he wanted so she could study Latin and keep up with her *triggeronomy*.

35, 35, 35.

I thought about the money he wanted for the tutor all the rest of that week, and over the weekend, too. Sometimes I took out those two bills – I had unfolded them but the creases still remained – and studied at them. On Sunday night I made my decision. I told Henry that he'd have to take the Model T to school on Monday; I had to go to Hemingford Home and see Mr Stoppenhauser at the bank about a shortie loan. A small one. Just 35 dollars.

'What for?' Henry was sitting at the window and looking moodily out at the darkening West Field.

I told him. I thought it would start another argument about Shannon, and in a way, I wanted that. He'd said nothing about her all week, although I knew Shan was gone. Mert Donovan had told me when he came by for a load of seed corn. 'Went off to some fancy school back in Omaha,' he said. 'Well, more power to her, that's what I think. If they're gonna vote, they better learn. Although,' he added after a moment's cogitation, 'mine does what I tell her. She better, if she knows what's good for her.'

If I knew she was gone, Henry also knew, and probably before I did – schoolchildren are enthusiastic gossips. But he had said nothing. I suppose I was trying to give him a reason to let out all the hurt and recriminations.

It wouldn't be pleasant, but in the long run it might be beneficial. Neither a sore on the forehead or in the brain behind the forehead should be allowed to fester. If they do, the infection is likely to spread.

But he only grunted at the news, so I decided to poke a little harder.

'You and I are going to split the payback,' I said. 'It's apt to come to no more than 38 dollars if we retire the loan by Christmas. That's 19 apiece. I'll take yours out of your choring money.'

Surely, I thought, this would result in a flood of anger . . . but it brought only another surly little grunt. He didn't even argue about having to take the Model T to school, although he said the other kids made fun of it, calling it 'Hank's ass-breaker.'

'Son?'

'What.'

'Are you all right?'

He turned to me and smiled – his lips moved around, at least. 'I'm fine. Good luck at the bank tomorrow, Poppa. I'm going to bed.'

As he stood up, I said: 'Will you give me a little kiss?'

He kissed my cheek. It was the last one.

He took the T to school and I drove the truck to Hemingford Home, where Mr Stoppenhauser brought me into his office after a mere five-minute wait. I explained what I needed, but declined to say what I needed it for, only citing personal reasons. I thought for such a piddling amount I would not need to be more specific, and I was right. But when I'd finished, he folded his hands on his desk blotter and gave me a look of almost fatherly sternness. In the corner, the Regulator clock ticked away quiet slices of time. On the street – considerably louder – came the blat of an engine. It stopped, there was silence, and then another engine started up. Was that my son, first arriving in the Model T and then stealing my truck? There's no way I can know for sure, but I think it was.

'Wilf,' Mr Stoppenhauser said, 'you've had a little time to get over your wife leaving the way she did — pardon me for bringing up a painful subject, but it seems pertinent, and besides, a banker's office is a little like a priest's confessional — so I'm going to talk to you like a Dutch uncle. Which is only fitting, since that's where my mother and father came from.'

I had heard this one before — as had, I imagine, most visitors to that office — and I gave it the dutiful smile it was meant to elicit.

'Will Home Bank & Trust loan you 35 dollars? You bet. I'm tempted to put it on a man-to-man basis and do the deal out of my own wallet, except I never carry more than what it takes to pay for my lunch at the Splendid Diner and a shoe-shine at the barber shop. Too much money's a constant temptation, even for a wily old cuss like me, and besides, business is business. *But!*' He raised his finger. 'You don't *need* 35 dollars.'

'Sad to say, I do.' I wondered if he knew why. He might have; he was indeed a wily old cuss. But so was Harl Cotterie, and Harl was also a shamed old cuss that fall.

'No; you don't. You need 750, that's what you need, and you could have it today. Either bank it or walk out with it in your pocket, all the same to me either way. You paid off the mortgage on your place 3 years ago. It's free and clear. So there's absolutely no reason why you shouldn't turn around and take out another mortgage. It's done all the time, my boy, and by the best people. You'd be surprised at some of the paper we're carrying. All the best people. Yessir.'

'I thank you very kindly, Mr Stoppenhauser, but

I don't think so. That mortgage was like a gray cloud over my head the whole time it was in force, and—'

'Wilf, that's the *point*!' The finger went up again. This time it wagged back and forth, like the pendulum of the Regulator. 'That is exactly the rootin'-tootin', cowboy-shootin' *point*! It's the fellows who take out a mortgage and then feel like they're always walking around in sunshine who end up defaulting and losing their valuable property! Fellows like you, who carry that bank-paper like a barrowload of rocks on a gloomy day, are the fellows who always pay back! And do you want to tell me that there aren't improvements you could make? A roof to fix? A little more livestock?' He gave me a sly and roguish look. 'Maybe even indoor plumbing, like your neighbor down the road? Such things pay for themselves, you know. You could end up with improvements that far outweigh the cost of a mortgage. Value for money, Wilf! Value for money!'

I thought it over. At last I said, 'I'm very tempted, sir. I won't lie about that—'

'No need to. A banker's office, the priest's confessional – very little difference. The best men in this county have sat in that chair, Wilf. The very best.'

'But I only came in for a shortie loan – which you have kindly granted – and this new proposal needs a little thinking about.' A new idea occurred to me, one that was surprisingly pleasant. 'And I ought to talk it over with my boy, Henry – Hank, as he likes to be called now. He's getting to an age where he needs to be consulted, because what I've got will be his someday.'

'Understood, completely understood. But it's the right thing to do, believe me.' He got to his feet and stuck out his hand. I got to mine and shook it. 'You came in here to buy a fish, Wilf. I'm offering to sell you a pole. Much better deal.'

'Thank you.' And, leaving the bank, I thought: *I'll talk it over with my son.* It was a good thought. A warm thought in a heart that had been chilly for months.

The mind is a funny thing, isn't it? Preoccupied as I was by Mr Stoppenhauser's unsolicited offer of a mortgage, I never noticed that the vehicle I'd come in had been replaced by the one Henry had taken to school. I'm not sure I would have noticed right away even if I'd had less weighty matters on my mind. They were both familiar to me, after all; they were both mine. I only realized when I was leaning in to get the crank and saw a folded piece of paper, held down by a rock, on the driving seat.

I just stood there for a moment, half in and half out of the T, one hand on the side of the cab, the other reaching under the seat, which was where we kept the crank. I suppose I knew why Henry had left school and made this swap even before I pulled his note from beneath the makeshift paper-weight and unfolded it. The truck was more reliable on a long trip. A trip to Omaha, for instance.

> *Poppa,*
>
> *I have taken the truck. I guess you know where I am going. Leave me alone. I know you can send Sheriff Jones after me to bring me back, but if you do I will tell everything. You might think I'd change my mind because I am 'just a kid,' BUT I WONT. Without Shan I dont care about nothing. I love you Poppa even if I don't know why, since everything we did has brought me mizzery.*
>
> *Your Loving Son,*
> *Henry 'Hank' James*

I drove back to the farm in a daze. I think some people waved to me – I think even Sallie Cotterie, who was minding the Cotteries' roadside vegetable stand, waved to me – and I probably waved back, but I've no memory of doing so. For the first time since Sheriff Jones had come out to the farm, asking his cheerful, no-answers-needed questions and looking at everything with his cold inquisitive eyes, the electric chair seemed like a real possibility to me, so real I could almost feel the buckles on my skin as the leather straps were tightened on my wrists and above my elbows.

He would be caught whether I kept my mouth shut or not. That seemed inevitable to me. He had no money, not even six bits to fill the truck's gas tank, so he'd be walking long before he even got to Elkhorn. If he managed to steal some gas, he'd be caught when he approached the place where she was now living (Henry assumed as a prisoner; it had never crossed his unfinished mind that she might be a willing guest). Surely Harlan had given the person in charge – Sister Camilla – Henry's description. Even if he hadn't considered the possibility of the outraged swain making an appearance at the site of his lady-love's durance vile, Sister Camilla would have. In her business, she had surely dealt with outraged swains before.

My only hope was that, once accosted by the authorities, Henry would keep silent long enough to realize that he'd been snared by his own foolishly romantic notions rather than by my interference. Hoping for a teenage boy to come to his senses is like betting on a long shot at the horse track, but what else did I have?

As I drove into the dooryard, a wild thought crossed my mind: leave the T running, pack a bag, and take off for Colorado. The idea lived for no more than two seconds. I had money – 75 dollars, in fact – but the T would die long before I crossed the state line at Julesburg. And that wasn't the important thing; if it had been, I could always have driven as far as Lincoln and then traded the T and

60 of my dollars for a reliable car. No, it was the place. The home place. *My* home place. I had murdered my wife to keep it, and I wasn't going to leave it now because my foolish and immature accomplice had gotten it into his head to take off on a romantic quest. If I left the farm, it wouldn't be for Colorado; it would be for state prison. And I would be taken there in chains.

That was Monday. There was no word on Tuesday or Wednesday. Sheriff Jones didn't come to tell me Henry had been picked up hitchhiking on the Lincoln-Omaha Highway, and Harl Cotterie didn't come to tell me (with Puritanical satisfaction, no doubt), that the Omaha police had arrested Henry at Sister Camilla's request, and he was currently sitting in the pokey, telling wild tales about knives and wells and burlap bags. All was quiet on the farm. I worked in the garden harvesting pantry-vegetables, I mended fences, I milked the cows, I fed the chickens – and I did it all in a daze. Part of me, and not a small part, either, believed that all of this was a long and terribly complex dream from which I would awake with Arlette snoring beside me and the sound of Henry chopping wood for the morning fire.

Then, on Thursday, Mrs McReady – the dear and portly widow who taught academic subjects at Hemingford School – came by in her own Model T to ask me if Henry was all right. 'There's an . . . an intestinal *distress* going around,' she said. 'I wondered if he caught it. He left very suddenly.'

'He's distressed all right,' I said, 'but it's a love-bug instead of a stomach-bug. He's run off, Mrs McReady.' Unexpected tears, stinging and hot, rose in my eyes. I took the handkerchief from the pocket on the front of my biballs, but some of them ran down my cheeks before I could wipe them away.

When my vision was clear again, I saw that Mrs McReady, who meant well by every child, even the difficult ones, was near tears herself. She must have known all along what kind of bug Henry was suffering from.

'He'll be back, Mr James. Don't you fear. I've seen this before, and I expect to see it a time or two again before I retire, although that time's not so far away as it once was.' She lowered her voice, as if she feared George the rooster or one of his feathered harem might be a spy. 'The one you want to watch out for is her father. He's a hard and unbending man. Not a bad man, but hard.'

'I know,' I said. 'And I suppose you know where his daughter is now.'

She lowered her eyes. It was answer enough.

'Thank you for coming out, Mrs McReady. Can I ask you to keep this to yourself?'

'Of course . . . but the children are already whispering.'

Yes. They would be.

'Are you on the exchange, Mr James?' She looked for telephone wires. 'I see you are not. Never mind. If I hear anything, I'll come out and tell you.'

'You mean if you hear anything before Harlan Cotterie or Sheriff Jones.'

'God will take care of your son. Shannon, too. You know, they really were a lovely couple; everyone said so. Sometimes the fruit ripens too early, and a frost kills it. Such a shame. Such a sad, sad shame.'

She shook my hand – a man's strong grip – and then drove away in her flivver. I don't think she realized that, at the end, she had spoken of Shannon and my son in the past tense.

On Friday Sheriff Jones came out, driving the car with the gold star on the door. And he wasn't alone. Following along behind was my truck. My heart leaped at the sight of it, then sank again when I saw who was behind the wheel: Lars Olsen.

I tried to wait quietly while Jones went through his Ritual of Arrival: belt-hitching, forehead-wiping (even though the day was chilly and overcast), hair-brushing. I couldn't do it. 'Is he all right? Did you find him?'

'No, nope, can't say we did.' He mounted the porch steps. 'Line-rider over east of Lyme Biska found the truck, but no sign of the kid. We might know better about the state of his health if you'd reported this when it happened. Wouldn't we?'

'I was hoping he'd come back on his own,' I said dully. 'He's gone to Omaha. I don't know how much I need to tell you, Sheriff—'

Lars Olsen had meandered into auditory range, ears all but flapping. 'Go on back to my car, Olsen,' Jones said. 'This is a private conversation.'

Lars, a meek soul, scurried off without demur. Jones turned back to me. He was far less cheerful than on his previous visit, and had dispensed with the bumbling persona, as well.

'I already know enough, don't I? That your kid got Harl Cotterie's daughter in the fam'ly way and has probably gone haring off to Omaha. He run the truck off the road into a field of high grass when he knew the tank was 'bout dry. That was smart. He get that kind of smart from you? Or from Arlette?'

I said nothing, but he'd given me an idea. Just a little one, but it might come in handy.

'I'll tell you one thing he did that we'll thank him for,' Jones said. 'Might keep him out of jail, too. He yanked all the grass from under the truck before he went on his merry way. So the exhaust wouldn't catch it afire, you know. Start a big prairie fire that burned a couple thousand acres, a jury might get a bit touchy, don't you think? Even if the offender was only 15 or so?'

'Well, it didn't happen, Sheriff – he did the right thing – so why are you going on about it?' I knew the answer, of course. Sheriff Jones might not give a hoot in a high wind for the likes of Andrew Lester, attorney-at-law, but he was good friends with Harl. They were both members of the newly formed Elks Lodge, and Harl had it in for my son.

'A little touchy, aren't you?' He wiped his forehead again, then resettled his Stetson. 'Well, I might be touchy, too, if it was my son. And you know what? If it was my son and Harl Cotterie was my neighbor – my *good* neighbor – I might've just taken a run down there and said, "Harl? You know what? I think my son might be going to try and see your daughter. You want to tell someone to be on the peep for him?" But you didn't do that, either, did you?'

The idea he'd given me was looking better and better, and it was almost time to spring it.

'He hasn't shown up wherever she is, has he?'

'Not yet, no, he may still be looking for it.'

'I don't think he ran away to see Shannon,' I said.

'Why, then? Do they have a better brand of icecream there in Omaha? Because that's the way he was headed, sure as your life.'

'I think he went looking for his mother. I think she may have gotten in touch with him.'

That stopped him for a good ten seconds, long enough for a wipe of the forehead and a brush of the hair. Then he said, 'How would she do that?'

'A letter would be my best guess.' The Hemingford Home Grocery was also the post office, where all the general delivery went. 'They would have given it to him when he went in for candy or a bag of peanuts, as he often does on his way back from school. I don't know for sure, Sheriff, anymore than I know why you came out here acting like I committed some kind of crime. I wasn't the one who knocked her up.'

'You ought to hush that kind of talk about a nice girl!'

'Maybe yes and maybe no, but this was as much a surprise to me as it was to the Cotteries, and now my boy is gone. They at least know where their daughter is.'

Once again he was stumped. Then he took out a little notebook from his back pocket and jotted something in it. He put it back and asked, 'You don't know for sure that your wife got in touch with your kid, though – that's what you're telling me? It's just a guess?'

'I know he talked a lot about his mother after she left, but then he stopped. And I know he hasn't shown up at that home where Harlan and his wife stuck Shannon.' And on that score I was as surprised as Sheriff Jones . . . but awfully grateful. 'Put the two things together, and what do you get?'

'I don't know,' Jones said, frowning. 'I truly don't. I thought I had this figured out, but I've been wrong before, haven't I? Yes, and will be again. "We are all bound in error," that's what the Book says. But good God, kids make my life hard. If you hear from your son, Wilfred, I'd tell him to get his skinny ass home and stay away from Shannon Cotterie, if he knows where she is. She won't want to see him, guarantee you that. Good news is no prairie fire, and we can't arrest him for stealing his father's truck.'

'No,' I said grimly, 'you'd never get me to press charges on that one.'

'*But*.' He raised his finger, which reminded me of Mr Stoppenhauser at the bank. 'Three days ago, in Lyme Biska – not so far from where the rider found your truck – someone held up that grocery and ethyl station on the edge of town. The one with the Blue Bonnet Girl on the roof? Took 23 dollars. I got the report sitting on my desk. It was a young fella dressed in old cowboy clothes, with a bandanna pulled up over his mouth and a plainsman hat slouched down over his eyes. The owner's mother was tending the counter, and the fella menaced her with some sort of tool. She thought it might have been a crowbar or a pry-rod, but who knows? She's pushing 80 and half-blind.'

It was my time to be silent. I was flabbergasted. At last I said, 'Henry left from school, Sheriff, and so far as I can remember he was wearing a flannel shirt and corduroy trousers that day. He didn't take any of his clothes, and in any case he doesn't *have* any cowboy clothes, if you mean boots and all. Nor does he have a plainsman's hat.'

'He could have stolen those things, too, couldn't he?'

'If you don't know anything more than what you just said, you ought to stop. I know you're friends with Harlan—'

'Now, now, this has nothing to do with that.'

It did and we both knew it, but there was no reason to go any farther down that road. Maybe my 80 acres didn't stack up very high against Harlan Cotterie's 400, but I was still a landowner and a taxpayer, and I wasn't going to be browbeaten. That was the point I was making, and Sheriff Jones had taken it.

'My son's not a robber, and he doesn't threaten women. That's not how he acts and not the way he was raised.'

Not until just lately, anyway, a voice inside whispered.

'Probably just a drifter looking for a quick payday,' Jones said. 'But I felt like I had to bring it up, and so I did. And we don't know what people might say, do we? Talk gets around. Everybody talks, don't they? Talk's cheap. The subject's closed as far as I'm concerned – let the Lyme County Sheriff worry about what goes on in Lyme Biska, that's my motto – but you should know that the Omaha police are keeping an eye on the place where Shannon Cotterie's at. Just in case your son gets in touch, you know.'

He brushed back his hair, then resettled his hat a final time.

'Maybe he'll come back on his own, no harm done, and we can write this whole thing off as, I don't know, a bad debt.'

'Fine. Just don't call him a bad son, unless you're willing to call Shannon Cotterie a bad daughter.'

The way his nostrils flared suggested he didn't like that much, but he didn't reply to it. What he said was, 'If he comes back and says he's seen his mother, let me know, would you? We've got her on the books as a missing person. Silly, I know, but the law is the law.'

'I'll do that, of course.'

He nodded and went to his car. Lars had settled behind the wheel. Jones shooed him over – the Sheriff was the kind of man who did his own driving. I thought about the young man who'd held up the store, and tried to tell myself that my Henry would never do such a thing, and even if he were driven to it, he wouldn't be sly enough to put on clothes he'd stolen out of somebody's barn or bunkhouse. But Henry was different now, and murderers *learn* slyness, don't they? It's a survival skill. I thought that maybe—

But no. I won't say it that way. It's too weak. This is my confession, my last word on everything, and if I can't tell the truth, the whole truth, and nothing but the truth, what good is it? What good is anything?

It was him. It was Henry. I had seen by Sheriff Jones's eyes that he only brought up that side-o'-the-road robbery because I wouldn't kowtow to him the way he thought

I should've, but *I* believed it. Because I knew more than Sheriff Jones. After helping your father to murder your mother, what was stealing some new clothes and waving a crowbar in an old granny's face? No such much. And if he tried it once, he would try it again, once those 23 dollars were gone. Probably in Omaha. Where they would catch him. And then the whole thing might come out. Almost certainly *would* come out.

I climbed to the porch, sat down, and put my face in my hands.

Days went by. I don't know how many, only that they were rainy. When the rain comes in the fall, outside chores have to wait, and I didn't have enough livestock or outbuildings to fill the hours with inside chores. I tried to read, but the words wouldn't seem to string together, although every now and then a single one would seem to leap off the page and scream. Murder. Guilt. Betrayal. Words like those.

Days I sat on the porch with a book in my lap, bundled into my sheepskin coat against the damp and the cold, watching the rainwater drip off the overhang. Nights I lay awake until the small hours of the morning, listening to the rain on the roof overhead. It sounded like timid fingers tapping for entry. I spent too much time thinking about Arlette in the well with Elphis. I began to fancy that she was still . . . not alive (I was under stress but not crazy), but somehow *aware*. Somehow watching developments from her makeshift grave, and with pleasure.

Do you like how things have turned out, Wilf? she'd ask if she could (and, in my imagination, did). *Was it worth it? What do you say?*

One night about a week after Sheriff Jones's visit, as I sat trying to read *The House of the Seven Gables*, Arlette crept up behind me, reached around the side of my head, and tapped the bridge of my nose with one cold, wet finger.

I dropped the book on the braided sitting-room rug, screamed, and leaped to my feet. When I did, the cold fingertip ran down to the corner of my mouth. Then it touched me again, on top of my head, where the hair was getting thin. This time I laughed − a shaky, angry laugh − and bent to pick up my book. As I did, the finger tapped a third time, this one on the nape of the neck, as if my dead wife were saying, *Have I got your attention yet, Wilf?* I stepped away − so the fourth tap wouldn't be in the eye − and looked up. The ceiling overhead was discolored and dripping. The plaster hadn't started to bulge yet, but if the rain continued, it would. It might even dissolve and come down in chunks. The leak was above my special reading-place. Of course it was. The rest of the ceiling looked fine, at least so far.

I thought of Stoppenhauser saying, *Do you want to tell me there aren't improvements you could make? A roof to fix?* And that sly look. As if he had *known*. As if he and Arlette were in on it together.

Don't be getting such things in your head, I told myself. *Bad enough that you keep thinking of her, down there. Have the worms gotten her eyes yet, I wonder? Have the bugs eaten away her sharp tongue, or at least blunted it?*

I went to the table in the far corner of the room, got the bottle that stood there, and poured myself a good-sized hooker of brown whiskey. My hand trembled, but only a little. I downed it in two swallows. I knew it would be a bad business to turn such drinking into a habit, but it's not every night that a man feels his dead wife tap him on the nose. And the hooch made me feel better. More in control of myself. I didn't need to take on a 750-dollar mortgage to fix my roof, I could patch it with scrap lumber when the rain stopped. But it would be an ugly fix; would make the place look like what my mother would have called trash-poor. Nor was that the point. Fixing a leak would take only a day or two. I needed work that would keep me through the winter. Hard labour would drive out thoughts of Arlette on her dirt throne, Arlette in her burlap *snood*. I needed home improvement projects that would send me to bed so tired that I'd sleep right through, and not lie there listening to the rain and wondering if Henry was out in it, maybe coughing from the grippe. Sometimes work is the only thing, the only answer.

The next day I drove to town in my truck and did what I never would have thought of doing if I hadn't needed to borrow 35 dollars: I took out a mortgage for 750. In the end we are all caught in devices of our own making. I believe that. In the end we are all caught.

In Omaha that same week, a young man wearing a plainsman's hat walked into a pawnshop on Dodge Street and bought a nickel-plated .32 caliber pistol. He paid with 5 dollars that had no doubt been handed to him, under duress, by a half-blind old woman who did business beneath the sign of the Blue Bonnet Girl. The next day, a young man wearing a flat cap on his head and a red bandanna over his mouth and nose walked into the Omaha branch of the First Agricultural Bank, pointed a gun at a pretty young teller named Rhoda Penmark, and demanded all the money in her drawer. She passed over about 200 dollars, mostly in ones and fives – the grimy kind farmers carry rolled up in the pockets of their bib overalls.

As he left, stuffing the money into his pants with one hand (clearly nervous, he dropped several bills on the floor), the portly guard – a retired policeman – said: 'Son, you don't want to do this.'

The young man fired his .32 into the air. Several people screamed. 'I don't want to shoot you, either,' the young man said from behind his bandanna, 'but I will if I have to. Fall back against that post, sir, and stay there if you know what's good for you. I've got a friend outside watching the door.'

The young man ran out, already stripping the bandanna from his face. The guard waited for a minute or so, then went out with his hands raised (he had no sidearm), just in case there really was a friend. There wasn't, of course. Hank James had no friends in Omaha except for the one with his baby growing in her belly.

I took 200 dollars of my mortgage money in cash and left the rest in Mr Stoppenhauser's bank. I went shopping at the hardware, the lumberyard, and the grocery store where Henry might have gotten a letter from his mother . . . if she were still alive to write one. I drove out of town in a drizzle that had turned to slashing rain by the time I got home. I unloaded my newly purchased lumber and shingles, did the feeding and milking, then put away my groceries – mostly dry goods and staples that were running low without Arlette to ride herd on the kitchen. With that chore done, I put water on the woodstove to heat for a bath and stripped off my damp clothes. I pulled the wad of money out of the right front pocket of my crumpled biballs, counted it, and saw I still had just shy of 160 dollars. Why had I taken so much in cash? Because my mind had been elsewhere. *Where* elsewhere, pray? On Arlette and Henry, of course. Not to mention Henry and Arlette. They were pretty much all I thought about on those rainy days.

I knew it wasn't a good idea to have so much cash money around. It would have to go back to the bank, where it could earn a little interest (although not nearly enough to equal the interest on the loan) while I was thinking about how best to put it to work. But in the meantime, I should lay it by someplace safe.

The box with the red whore's hat in it came to mind. It was where she'd stashed her own money, and it had been safe there for God knew how long. There was too much in my wad to fit in the band, so I thought I'd put it in the hat itself. It would only be there until I found an excuse to go back to town.

I went into the bedroom, stark naked, and opened the closet door. I shoved aside the box with her white church-hat in it, then reached for the other one. I'd pushed it all the way to the back of the shelf and had to stand on tiptoe to reach it. There was an elastic cord around it. I hooked my finger under it to pull it forward, was momentarily aware that the hatbox felt much too heavy – as though there were a brick inside it instead of a bonnet – and then there was a strange *freezing* sensation, as though my hand had been doused in icewater. A moment later the freeze turned to fire. It was a pain so intense that it locked all the muscles in my arm. I stumbled backwards, roaring in surprise and agony and dropping money everywhere. My finger was still hooked into the elastic, and the hatbox came tumbling out. Crouched on top of it was a Norway rat that looked all too familiar.

You might say to me, 'Wilf, one rat looks like another,' and ordinarily you'd be right, but I knew this one; hadn't I seen it running away from me with a cow's teat jutting from its mouth like the butt of a cigar?

The hatbox came free of my bleeding hand, and the rat tumbled to the floor. If I had taken time to think, it would have gotten away again, but conscious thinking had been canceled by pain, surprise, and the horror I suppose almost any man feels when he sees blood pouring from a part of his body that was whole only seconds before. I didn't even remember that I was as naked as the day I was born, just brought my right foot down on the rat. I heard its bones crunch and felt its guts squash. Blood and liquefied intestines squirted from beneath its tail and doused my left ankle with warmth. It tried to twist around and bite me again; I could see its large front teeth gnashing, but it couldn't quite reach me. Not, that was, as long as I kept my foot on it. So I did. I pushed harder, holding my wounded hand against my chest, feeling the warm blood mat the thick pelt that grew there. The rat twisted and flopped. Its tail first lashed my calf, then wrapped around it like a grass snake. Blood gushed from its mouth. Its black eyes bulged like marbles.

I stood there with my foot on the dying rat for a long time. It was smashed to pieces inside, its innards reduced to gruel, and still it thrashed and tried to bite. Finally it stopped moving. I stood on it for another minute, wanting to make sure it wasn't just playing possum (a rat playing possum – ha!), and when I was sure it was dead, I limped into the kitchen, leaving bloody footprints and thinking in a confused way of the oracle warning Pelias to beware of a man wearing just one sandal. But I was no Jason; I was a farmer half-mad with pain and amazement, a farmer who seemed condemned to foul his sleeping-place with blood.

As I held my hand under the pump and froze it with cold water, I could hear someone saying, 'No more, no more, no more.' It was me, I knew it was, but it sounded like an old man. One who had been reduced to beggary.

I can remember the rest of that night, but it's like looking at old photographs in a mildewy album. The rat had bitten all the way through the webbing between my left thumb and forefinger – a terrible bite, but in a way, lucky. If it had seized on the finger I'd hooked under that elastic cord, it might have bitten the finger entirely off. I realized that when I went back into the bedroom and picked up my adversary by the tail (using my right hand; the left was too stiff and painful to flex). It was two feet long, a six-pounder, at least.

Then it wasn't the same rat that escaped into the pipe, I hear you saying. *It couldn't have been.* But it was, I tell you it was. There was no identifying mark – no white patch of fur or conveniently memorable chewed ear – but I knew it was the one that had savaged Achelois. Just as I knew it hadn't been crouched up there by accident.

I carried it into the kitchen by the tail and dumped it in the ash bucket. This I took out to our swill-pit. I was naked in the pouring rain, but hardly aware of it. What I was mostly aware of was my left hand, throbbing with a pain so intense it threatened to obliterate all thought.

I took my duster from the hook in the mudroom (it was all I could manage), shrugged into it, and went out again, this time into the barn. I smeared my wounded hand with Rawleigh Salve. It had kept Achelois's udder from infecting, and might do the same for my hand. I started to leave, then remembered how the rat had escaped me last time. The pipe! I went to it and bent over, expecting to see the cement plug either chewed to pieces or completely gone, but it was intact. Of course it was. Even six-pound rats with oversized teeth can't chew through concrete. That the idea had even crossed my mind shows the state I was in. For a moment I seemed to see myself as if from outside: a man naked except for an unbuttoned duster, his body-hair matted with blood all the way to the groin, his torn left hand glistening under a thick snot-like coating of cow-salve, his eyes bugging out of his head. The way the rat's had bugged out, when I stepped on it.

It wasn't the same rat, I told myself. *The one that bit Achelois is either lying dead in the pipe or in Arlette's lap.*

But I knew it was. I knew it then and I know it now.

It was.

Back in the bedroom, I got down on my knees and picked up the bloodstained money. It was slow work with only one hand. Once I bumped my torn hand on the side of the bed and howled with pain. I could see fresh blood staining the salve, turning it pink. I put the cash on the dresser, not even bothering to cover it with a book or one of Arlette's damned ornamental plates. I couldn't even remember why it had seemed so important to hide the bills in the first place. The red hatbox I kicked into the closet, and then slammed the door. It could stay there until the end of time, for all of me.

Anyone who's ever owned a farm or worked on one will tell you that accidents are commonplace, and precautions must be taken. I had a big roll of bandage in the chest beside the kitchen pump – the chest Arlette had always called the 'hurt-locker.' I started to get the roll out, but then the big pot steaming on the stove caught my eye. The water I'd put on for a bath when I was still whole and when such monstrous pain as that which seemed to be consuming me was only theoretical. It occurred to me that hot soapy water might be just the thing for my hand. The wound couldn't hurt any worse, I reasoned, and the immersion would cleanse it. I was wrong on both counts, but how was I to know? All these years later, it still seems like a reasonable idea. I suppose it might even have worked, if I had been bitten by an ordinary rat.

I used my good right hand to ladle hot water into a basin (the idea of tilting the pot and pouring from it was out of the question), then added a cake of Arlette's coarse brown washing soap. The last cake, as it turned out; there are so many supplies a man neglects to lay in when he's not used to doing it. I added a rag, then went into the bedroom, got down on my knees again, and began mopping up the blood and guts. All the time remembering (of course) the last time I had cleaned blood from the floor in that damned bedroom. That time at least Henry had been with me to share the horror. Doing it alone, and in pain, was a terrible job. My shadow bumped and flitted on the wall, making me think of Quasimodo in Hugo's *Notre-Dame de Paris*.

With the job almost finished, I stopped and cocked my head, breath held, eyes wide, my heart seeming to thud in my bitten left hand. I heard a *scuttering* sound, and it seemed to come from everywhere. The sound of running rats. In that moment I was sure of it. The rats from the well. Her loyal courtiers. They had found another way out. The one crouched on top of the red hatbox had only been the first and the boldest. They had infiltrated the house, they were in the walls, and soon they would come out and overwhelm me. She would have her revenge. I would hear her laughing as they tore me to pieces.

The wind gusted hard enough to shake the house and shriek briefly along the eaves. The scuttering sound intensified, then faded a bit when the wind died. The relief that filled me was so intense it overwhelmed the pain (for a few seconds, at least). It wasn't rats; it was sleet. With the coming of dark, the temperature had fallen and the rain had become semi-solid. I went back to scrubbing away the remains.

When I was done, I dumped the bloody wash-water over the porch rail, then went back to the barn to apply a fresh coating of salve to my hand. With the wound completely cleansed, I could see that the webbing between my thumb and forefinger was torn open in three slashes that looked like a sergeant's stripes. My left thumb hung askew, as if the rat's teeth had severed some important cable between it and the rest of my left hand. I applied the cow-goop and then plodded back to the house, thinking, *It hurts but at least it's clean. Achelois was all right;*

I'll be all right, too. Everything's fine. I tried to imagine my body's defenses mobilizing and arriving at the scene of the bite like tiny firemen in red hats and long canvas coats.

At the bottom of the hurt-locker, wrapped in a torn piece of silk that might once have been part of a lady's slip, I found a bottle of pills from the Hemingford Home Drug Store. Fountain-penned on the label in neat capital letters was **ARLETTE JAMES Take 1 or 2 at Bed-Time for Monthly Pain.** I took three, with a large shot of whiskey. I don't know what was in those pills – morphia, I suppose – but they did the trick. The pain was still there, but it seemed to belong to a Wilfred James currently existing on some other level of reality. My head swam; the ceiling began to turn gently above me; the image of tiny firemen arriving to douse the blaze of infection before it could take hold grew clearer. The wind was strengthening, and to my half-dreaming mind, the constant low rattle of sleet against the house sounded more like rats than ever, but I knew better. I think I even said so aloud: 'I know better, Arlette, you don't fool me.'

As consciousness dwindled and I began to slip away, I realized that I might be going for good: that the combination of shock, booze, and morphine might end my life. I would be found in a cold farmhouse, my skin blue-gray, my torn hand resting on my belly. The idea did not frighten me; on the contrary, it comforted me.

While I slept, the sleet turned to snow.

When I woke at dawn the following morning, the house was as chilly as a tomb and my hand had swelled up to twice its ordinary size. The flesh around the bite was ashy gray but the first three fingers had gone a dull pink that would be red by the end of the day. Touching anywhere on that hand except for the pinky caused excruciating pain. Nevertheless, I wrapped it as tightly as I could, and that reduced the throbbing. I got a fire started in the kitchen stove – one-handed it was a long job, but I managed – and then drew up close, trying to get warm. All of me except for the bitten hand, that was; that part of me was warm already. Warm and pulsing like a glove with a rat hiding inside it.

By midafternoon I was feverish, and my hand had swelled so tightly against the bandages that I had to loosen them. Just doing that made me cry out. I needed doctoring, but it was snowing harder than ever, and I wouldn't be able to get as far as Cotteries', let alone all the way to Hemingford Home. Even if the day had been clear and bright and dry, how would I ever have managed to crank the truck or the T with just one hand? I sat in the kitchen, feeding the stove until it roared like a dragon, pouring sweat and shaking with cold, holding my bandaged club of a hand to my chest, and remembering the way kindly Mrs McReady had surveyed my cluttered, not-particularly-prosperous dooryard. *Are you on the exchange, Mr James? I see you are not.*

No. I was not. I was by myself on the farm I had killed for, with no means of summoning help. I could see the flesh beginning to turn red beyond where the bandages stopped: at the wrist, full of veins that would carry the poison all through my body. The firemen had failed. I thought of tying the wrist off with elastics – of killing my left hand in an effort to save the rest of me – and even of amputating it with the hatchet we used to chop up kindling and behead the occasional chicken. Both ideas seemed perfectly plausible, but they also seemed like too much work. In the end I did nothing except hobble back to the hurt-locker for more of Arlette's pills. I took three more, this time with cold water – my throat was burning – and then resumed my seat by the fire. I was going to die of the bite. I was sure of it and resigned to it. Death from bites and infections was as common as dirt on the plains. If the pain became more than I could bear, I would swallow all the remaining pain-pills at once. What kept me from doing it right away – apart from the fear of death, which I suppose afflicts all of us, to a greater or lesser degree – was the possibility that someone might come: Harlan, or Sheriff Jones, or kindly Mrs McReady. It was even possible that Attorney Lester might show up to hector me some more about those God damned 100 acres.

But what I hoped most of all was that Henry might return. He didn't, though.

It was Arlette who came.

You may have wondered how I know about the gun Henry bought in the Dodge Street pawnshop, and the bank robbery in Jefferson Square. If you did, you probably said to yourself, *Well, it's a lot of time between 1922 and 1930; enough to fill in plenty of details at a library stocked with back issues of the* Omaha World-Herald.

I *did* go to the newspapers, of course. And I wrote to people who met my son and his pregnant girlfriend on their short, disastrous course from Nebraska to Nevada. Most of those people wrote back, willing enough to supply details. That sort of investigative work makes sense, and no doubt satisfies you. But those investigations came years later, after I left the farm, and only confirmed what I already knew.

Already? you ask, and I answer simply: *Yes. Already. And I knew it not just as it happened, but at least part of it before it happened. The last part of it.*

How? The answer is simple. My dead wife told me.

You disbelieve, of course. I understand that. Any rational person would. All I can do is reiterate that this is my confession, my last words on earth, and I've put nothing in it I don't know to be true.

*   *   *

I woke from a doze in front of the stove the following night (or the next; as the fever settled in, I lost track of time) and heard the rustling, scuttering sounds again. At first I assumed it had recommenced sleeting, but when I got up to tear a chunk of bread from the hardening loaf on the counter, I saw a thin orange sunset-streak on the horizon and Venus glowing in the sky. The storm was over, but the scuttering sounds were louder than ever. They weren't coming from the walls, however, but from the back porch.

The door-latch began moving. At first it only trembled, as if the hand trying to operate it was too weak to lift it entirely clear of the notch. The movement ceased, and I had just decided I hadn't seen it at all – that it was a delusion born of the fever – when it went all the way up with a little *clack* sound and the door swung open on a cold breath of wind. Standing on the porch was my wife. She was still wearing her burlap snood, now flecked with snow; it must have been a slow and painful journey from what should have been her final resting place. Her face was slack with decay, the lower half slewed to one side, her grin wider than ever. It was a knowing grin, and why not? The dead understand everything.

She was surrounded by her loyal court. It was they that had somehow gotten her out of the well. It was they that were holding her up. Without them, she would have been no more than a ghost, malevolent but helpless. But they had animated her. She was their queen; she was also their puppet. She came into the kitchen, moving with a horribly boneless gait that had nothing to do with walking. The rats scurried all around her, some looking up at her with love, some at me with hate. She swayed all the way around the kitchen, touring what had been her domain as clods fell from the skirt of her dress (there was no sign of the quilt or the counterpane) and her head bobbed and rolled on her cut throat. Once it tilted back all the way to her shoulder blades before snapping forward again with a low and fleshy smacking sound.

When she at last turned her cloudy eyes on me, I backed into the corner where the woodbox stood, now almost empty. 'Leave me alone,' I whispered. 'You aren't even here. You're in the well and you can't get out even if you're not dead.'

She made a gurgling noise – it sounded like someone choking on thick gravy – and kept coming, real enough to cast a shadow. And I could smell her decaying flesh, this woman who had sometimes put her tongue in my mouth during the throes of her passion. She was there. She was real. So was her royal retinue. I could feel them scurrying back and forth over my feet and tickling my ankles with their whiskers as they sniffed at the bottoms of my longjohn trousers.

My heels struck the woodbox, and when I tried to bend away from the approaching corpse, I overbalanced and sat down in it. I banged my swollen and infected hand, but hardly registered the pain. She was bending over me, and her face . . . *dangled*. The flesh had come loose from the bones and her face hung down like a face drawn on a child's balloon. A rat climbed the side of the woodbox, plopped onto my belly, ran up my chest, and sniffed at the underside of my chin. I could feel others scurrying around beneath my bent knees. But they didn't bite me. That particular task had already been accomplished.

She bent closer. The smell of her was overwhelming, and her cocked ear-to-ear grin . . . I can see it now, as I write. I told myself to die, but my heart kept pounding. Her hanging face slid alongside mine. I could feel my beard-stubble pulling off tiny bits of her skin; could hear her broken jaw grinding like a branch with ice on it. Then her cold lips were pressed against the burning, feverish cup of my ear, and she began whispering secrets that only a dead woman could know. I shrieked. I promised to kill myself and take her place in Hell if she would only stop. But she didn't. She wouldn't. The dead don't stop.

That's what I know now.

After fleeing the First Agricultural Bank with 200 dollars stuffed into his pocket (or probably more like 150 dollars; some of it went on the floor, remember), Henry disappeared for a little while. He 'laid low,' in the criminal parlance. I say this with a certain pride. I thought he would be caught almost immediately after he got to the city, but he proved me wrong. He was in love, he was desperate, he was still burning with guilt and horror over the crime he and I had committed . . . but in spite of those distractions (those *infections*), my son demonstrated bravery and cleverness, even a certain sad nobility. The thought of that last is the worst. It still fills me with melancholy for his wasted life (*three* wasted lives; I mustn't forget poor pregnant Shannon Cotterie) and shame for the ruination to which I led him, like a calf with a rope around its neck.

Arlette showed me the shack where he went to ground, and the bicycle stashed out back – that bicycle was the first thing he purchased with his stolen cash. I couldn't have told you then exactly where his hideout was, but in the years since I have located it and even visited it; just a side-o'-the-road lean-to with a fading Royal Crown Cola advertisement painted on the side. It was a few miles beyond Omaha's western outskirts and within sight of Boys Town, which had begun operating the year before. One room, a single glassless window, and no stove. He covered the bicycle with hay and weeds and laid his plans. Then, a week or so after robbing the First Agricultural Bank – by then police interest in a very minor robbery would have died down – he began making bicycle trips into Omaha.

A thick boy would have gone directly to the St Eusebia Catholic Home and been snared by the Omaha cops (as Sheriff Jones had no doubt expected he would be), but Henry Freeman James was smarter than that. He sussed out the Home's location, but didn't approach it. Instead, he looked for the nearest candy store and soda fountain. He correctly assumed that the girls would frequent it whenever they could (which was whenever their behavior merited a free afternoon and they had a little money in their bags), and although the St Eusebia girls weren't required to wear uniforms, they were easy enough to pick out by their dowdy dresses, downcast eyes, and their behavior – alternately flirty and skittish. Those with big bellies and no wedding rings would have been particularly conspicuous.

A thick boy would have attempted to strike up a conversation with one of these unfortunate daughters of Eve right there at the soda fountain, thus attracting attention. Henry took up a position outside, at the mouth of an alley running between the candy store and the notions shoppe next to it, sitting on a crate and reading the newspaper with his bike leaning against the brick next to him. He was waiting for a girl a little more adventurous than those content simply to sip their icecream sodas and then scuttle back to the sisters. That meant a girl who smoked. On his third afternoon in the alley, such a girl arrived.

I have found her since, and talked with her. There wasn't much detective work involved. I'm sure Omaha seemed like a metropolis to Henry and Shannon, but in 1922 it was really just a larger-than-average Midwestern town with city pretensions. Victoria Hallett is a respectable married woman with three children now, but in the fall of 1922, she was Victoria Stevenson: young, curious, rebellious, six months pregnant, and very fond of Sweet Caporals. She was happy enough to take one of Henry's when he offered her the pack.

'Take another couple for later,' he invited.

She laughed. 'I'd have to be a ding-dong to do that! The sisters search our bags and pull our pockets inside-out when we come back. I'll have to chew three sticks of Black Jack just to get the smell of this one fag off my breath.' She patted her bulging tummy with amusement and defiance. 'I'm in trouble, as I guess you can see. Bad girl! And my sweetie ran off. Bad *boy*, but the world don't care about that! So then the dapper stuck me in a jail with penguins for guards—'

'I don't get you.'

'Jeez! The dapper's my dad! And penguins is what we call the sisters!' She laughed. 'You're some country palooka, all right! And how! *Anyway*, the jail where I'm doing time's called—'

'St Eusebia's.'

'*Now* you're cooking with gas, Jackson.' She puffed her cig, narrowed her eyes. 'Say, I bet I know who you are – Shan Cotterie's boyfriend.'

'Give that girl a Kewpie doll,' Hank said.

'Well, I wouldn't get within two blocks of our place, that's my advice. The cops have got your description.' She laughed cheerily. 'Yours and half a dozen other Lonesome Lennies, but none of 'em green-eyed clodhoppers like you, and none with gals as good-looking as Shannon. She's a real Sheba! Yow!'

'Why do you think I'm here instead of there?'

'I'll bite – why *are* you here?'

'I want to get in touch, but I don't want to get caught doing it. I'll give you 2 bucks to take a note to her.'

Victoria's eyes went wide. 'Buddy, for a 2-spot, I'd tuck a bugle under my arm and take a message to Garcia – that's how tapped out I am. Hand it over!'

'And another 2 if you keep your mouth shut about it. Now and later.'

'For that you don't have to pay extra,' she said. 'I love pulling the business on those holier-than-thou bitches. Why, they smack your hand if you try to take an extra dinner roll! It's like *Gulliver Twist*!'

He gave her the note, and Victoria gave it to Shannon. It was in her little bag of things when the police finally caught up with her and Henry in Elko, Nevada, and I have seen a police photograph of it. But Arlette told me what it said long before then, and the actual item matched word for word.

I'll wait from midnight to dawn behind yr place every night for 2 weeks, the note said. *If you don't show up, I'll know it's over between us & go back to Hemingford & never bother you again even tho' I will go on loving you forever. We are young but we could lie about our ages & start a good life in another place (California). I have some money & know how to get more. Victoria knows how to find me if you want to send me a note, but only once. More would not be safe.*

I suppose Harlan and Sallie Cotterie might have that note. If so, they have seen that my son signed his name in a heart. I wonder if that was what convinced Shannon. I wonder if she even needed convincing. It's possible that all she wanted on earth was to keep (and legitimize) a baby she had already fallen in love with. That's a question Arlette's terrible whispering voice never addressed. Probably she didn't care one way or the other.

Henry returned to the mouth of the alley every day after that meeting. I'm sure he knew that the cops might arrive instead of Victoria, but felt he had no choice. On the third day of his vigil, she came. 'Shan wrote back right away, but I couldn't get out any sooner,' she said. 'Some goofy-weed showed up in that hole they have the nerve to call a music room, and the penguins have been on the warpath ever since.'

Henry held out his hand for the note, which Victoria gave over in exchange for a Sweet Caporal. There were only four words: *Tomorrow morning. 2 o'clock.*

Henry threw his arms around Victoria and kissed her. She laughed with excitement, eyes sparkling. 'Gosh! Some girls get all the luck.'

They undoubtedly do. But when you consider that Victoria ended up with a husband, three kids, and a nice home on Maple Street in the best part of Omaha, and Shannon Cotterie didn't live out that curse of a year . . . which of them would *you* say struck lucky?

I have some money & know how to get more, Henry had written, and he did. Only hours after kissing the saucy Victoria (who took the message *He says he'll be there with bells on* back to Shannon), a young man with a flat cap pulled low on his forehead and a bandanna over his mouth and nose robbed the First National Bank of Omaha. This time the robber got 800 dollars, which was a fine haul. But the guard was younger and more enthusiastic about his responsibilities, which was not so fine. The thief had to shoot him in the thigh in order to effect his escape, and although Charles Griner lived, an infection set in (I could sympathize), and he lost the leg. When I met with him at his parents' house in the spring of 1925, Griner was philosophical about it.

'I'm lucky to be alive at all,' he said. 'By the time they got a tourniquet on my leg, I was lying in a pool of blood damn near an inch deep. I bet it took a whole box of Dreft to get *that* mess up.'

When I tried to apologize for my son, he waved it away.

'I never should have approached him. The cap was

pulled low and the bandanna was yanked high, but I could see his eyes all right. I should have known he wasn't going to stop unless he was shot down, and I never had a chance to pull my gun. It was in his eyes, see. But I was young myself. I'm older now. Older's something your son never got a chance to get. I'm sorry for your loss.'

After that job, Henry had more than enough money to buy a car – a nice one, a tourer – but he knew better. (Writing that, I again feel that sense of pride: low but undeniable.) A kid who looked like he only started shaving a week or two before, waving around enough wampum to buy an almost-new Olds? That would have brought John Law down on him for sure.

So instead of buying a car, he stole one. Not a touring car, either; he plumped for a nice, nondescript Ford coupe. That was the car he parked behind St Eusebia's, and that was the one Shannon climbed into, after sneaking out of her room, creeping downstairs with her traveling bag in her hand, and wriggling through the window of the washroom adjacent to the kitchen. They had time to exchange a single kiss – Arlette didn't say so, but I still have my imagination – and then Henry pointed the Ford west. By dawn they were on the Omaha-Lincoln Highway. They must have passed close to his old home – and hers – around 3 that afternoon. They might have looked in that direction, but I doubt if Henry slowed; he would not want to stop for the night in an area where they might be recognized.

Their life as fugitives had begun.

Arlette whispered more about that life than I wished to know, and I don't have the heart to put more than the bare details down here. If you want to know more, write to the Omaha Public Library. For a fee, they will send you hectograph copies of stories having to do with the Sweetheart Bandits, as they became known (and as they called themselves). You may even be able to find stories from your own paper, if you do not live in Omaha; the conclusion of the tale was deemed heartrending enough to warrant national coverage.

Handsome Hank and Sweet Shannon, the *World-Herald* called them. In the photographs, they looked impossibly young. And of course they were. I didn't want to look at those photographs, but I did. There's more than one way to be bitten by rats, isn't there?

The stolen car blew a tire in Nebraska's sandhill country. Two men came walking up just as Henry was mounting the spare. One drew a shotgun from a sling setup he had under his coat – what was called a bandit hammerclaw back in the Wild West days – and pointed it at the runaway lovers. Henry had no chance at all to get his own gun; it was in his coat pocket, and if he'd tried for it, he almost certainly would have been killed. So the robber was robbed. Henry and Shannon walked hand-in-hand to a nearby farmer's house under a cold autumn sky, and when the farmer came to the door to ask how he could help, Henry pointed his gun at the man's chest and said he wanted his car and all his cash.

The girl with him, the farmer told a reporter, stood on the porch looking away. The farmer said he thought she was crying. He said he felt sorry for her, because she was no bigger than a minute, just as pregnant as the old woman who lived in a shoe, and traveling with a young desperado bound for a bad end.

Did she try to stop him? the reporter asked. Try to talk him out of it?

No, the farmer said. Just stood with her back turned, like she thought that if she didn't see it, it wasn't happening. The farmer's old rattletrap Reo was found abandoned near the McCook train depot, with a note on the seat: *Here is your car back, we will send the money we stole when*

we can. We only took from you because we were in a scrape.
Very truly yours, 'The Sweetheart Bandits.' Whose idea was
that name? Shannon's, probably; the note was in her
handwriting. They only used it because they didn't want
to give their names, but of such things legends are made.

A day or two later, there was a hold-up in the tiny
Frontier Bank of Arapahoe, Colorado. The thief – wearing
a flat cap yanked low and a bandanna yanked high – was
alone. He got less than 100 dollars and drove off in a
Hupmobile that had been reported stolen in McCook.
The next day, in The First Bank of Cheyenne Wells (which
was the only bank of Cheyenne Wells), the young man
was joined by a young woman. She disguised her face
with a bandanna of her own, but it was impossible to
disguise her pregnant state. They made off with 400 dollars
and drove out of town at high speed, headed west. A
roadblock was set up on the road to Denver, but Henry
played it smart and stayed lucky. They turned south not
long after leaving Cheyenne Wells, picking their way along
dirt roads and cattle tracks.

A week later, a young couple calling themselves Harry
and Susan Freeman boarded the train for San Francisco in
Colorado Springs. Why they suddenly got off in Grand
Junction I don't know and Arlette didn't say – saw something
that put their wind up, I suppose. All I know is that they
robbed a bank there, and another in Ogden, Utah. Their
version of saving up money for their new life, maybe. And
in Ogden, when a man tried to stop Henry outside the
bank, Henry shot him in the chest. The man grappled with
Henry anyway, and Shannon pushed him down the granite
steps. They got away. The man Henry shot died in the
hospital two days later. The Sweetheart Bandits had become
murderers. In Utah, convicted murderers got the rope.

By then it was near Thanksgiving, although which
side of it I don't know. The police west of the Rockies

had their descriptions and were on the lookout. I had been bitten by the rat hiding in the closet – I think – or was about to be. Arlette told me they were dead, but they weren't; not when she and her royal court came to visit me, that was. She either lied or prophesied. To me they are both the same.

Their next-to-last stop was Deeth, Nevada. It was a bitterly cold day in late November or early December, the sky white and beginning to spit snow. They only wanted eggs and coffee at the town's only diner, but their luck was almost all gone. The counterman was from Elkhorn, Nebraska, and although he hadn't been home in years, his mother still faithfully sent him issues of the *World-Herald* in large bundles. He had received just such a bundle a few days before, and he recognized the Omaha Sweetheart Bandits sitting in one of the booths.

Instead of ringing the police (or pit security at the nearby copper mine, which would have been quicker and more efficient), he decided to make a citizen's arrest. He took a rusty old cowboy pistol from under the counter, pointed it at them, and told them – in the finest Western tradition – to throw up their hands. Henry did no such thing. He slid out of the booth and walked toward the fellow, saying: 'Don't do that, my friend, we mean you no harm, we'll just pay up and go.'

The counterman pulled the trigger and the old pistol misfired. Henry took it out of his hand, broke it, looked at the cylinder, and laughed. 'Good news!' he told Shannon. 'These bullets have been in there so long they're green.'

He put 2 dollars on the counter – for their food – and then made a terrible mistake. To this day I believe things would have ended badly for them no matter what, yet still I wish I could call to him across the years: *Don't put that gun down still loaded. Don't do that, Son! Green or not, put those bullets in your pocket!* But only the dead can call across time; I know that now, and from personal experience.

As they were leaving (*hand-in-hand*, Arlette whispered in my burning ear), the counterman snatched that old horse-pistol off the counter, held it in both hands, and pulled the trigger again. This time it fired, and although he probably thought he was aiming at Henry, the bullet struck Shannon Cotterie in the lower back. She screamed and stumbled forward out the door into the blowing snow. Henry caught her before she could fall and helped her into their last stolen car, another Ford. The counterman tried to shoot him through the window, and that time the old gun blew up in his hands. A piece of metal took out his left eye. I have never been sorry. I am not as forgiving as Charles Griner.

Seriously wounded – perhaps dying already – Shannon went into labor as Henry drove through thickening snow toward Elko, thirty miles to the southwest, perhaps thinking he might find a doctor there. I don't know if there was a doctor or not, but there was certainly a police station, and the counterman rang it with the remains of his eyeball still drying on his cheek. Two local cops and four members of the Nevada State Patrol were waiting for Henry and Shannon at the edge of town, but Henry and Shannon never saw them. It's 30 miles between Deeth and Elko, and Henry made only 28 of them.

Just inside the town limits (but still well beyond the edge of the village), the last of Henry's luck let go. With Shannon screaming and holding her belly as she bled all over the seat, he must have been driving fast – too fast. Or maybe he just hit a pothole in the road. However it was, the Ford skidded into the ditch and stalled. There they sat in that high-desert emptiness while a strengthening wind blew snow all around them, and what was Henry thinking? That what he and I had done in Nebraska had led him and the girl he loved to that place in Nevada. Arlette didn't tell me that, but she didn't have to. I knew.

He spied the ghost of a building through the thickening snow, and got Shannon out of the car. She managed a few steps into the wind, then could manage no more. The girl who could do triggeronomy and might have been the first female graduate of the normal school in Omaha laid her head on her young man's shoulder and said, 'I can't go any farther, honey, put me on the ground.'

'What about the baby?' he asked her.

'The baby is dead, and I want to die, too,' she said. 'I can't stand the pain. It's terrible. I love you, honey, but put me on the ground.'

He carried her to that ghost of a building instead, which turned out to be a line shack not much different from the shanty near Boys Town, the one with the faded bottle of Royal Crown Cola painted on the side. There was a stove, but no wood. He went out and scrounged a few pieces of scrap lumber before the snow could cover them, and when he went back inside, Shannon was unconscious. Henry lit the stove, then put her head on his lap. Shannon Cotterie was dead before the little fire he'd made burned down to embers, and then there was only Henry, sitting on a mean lineshack cot where a dozen dirty cowboys had lain themselves down before him, drunk more often than sober. He sat there and stroked Shannon's hair while the wind shrieked outside and the shack's tin roof shivered.

All these things Arlette told me on a day when those two doomed children were still alive. All these things she told me while the rats crawled around me and her stink filled my nose and my infected, swollen hand ached like fire.

I begged her to kill me, to open my throat as I had opened hers, and she wouldn't.

That was her revenge.

It might have been two days later when my visitor arrived at the farm, or even three, but I don't think so. I think it was only one. I don't believe I could have lasted two or three more days without help. I had stopped eating and almost stopped drinking. Still, I managed to get out of bed and stagger to the door when the hammering on it commenced. Part of me thought it might be Henry, because part of me still dared hope that Arlette's visit had been a delusion hatched in delirium . . . and even if it had been real, that she had lied.

It was Sheriff Jones. My knees loosened when I saw him, and I pitched forward. If he hadn't caught me, I would have gone tumbling out onto the porch. I tried to tell him about Henry and Shannon – that Shannon was going to be shot, that they were going to end up in a line shack on the outskirts of Elko, that he, Sheriff Jones, had to call somebody and stop it before it happened. All that came out was a garble, but he caught the names.

'He's run off with her, all right,' Jones said. 'But if Harl came down and told you that, why'd he leave you like *this*? What bit you?'

'Rat,' I managed.

He got an arm around me and half-carried me down the porch steps and toward his car. George the rooster was lying frozen to the ground beside the woodpile, and the cows were lowing. When had I last fed them? I couldn't remember.

'Sheriff, you have to—'

But he cut me off. He thought I was raving, and why not? He could feel the fever baking off me and see it glowing in my face. It must have been like carrying an oven. 'You need to save your strength. And you need to be grateful to Arlette, because I never would have come out here if not for her.'

'Dead,' I managed.

'Yes. She's dead, all right.'

So then I told him I'd killed her, and oh, the relief. A plugged pipe inside my head had magically opened, and the infected ghost which had been trapped in there was finally gone.

He slung me into his car like a bag of meal. 'We'll talk about Arlette, but right now I'm taking you to Angels of Mercy, and I'll thank you not to upchuck in my car.'

As he drove out of the dooryard, leaving the dead rooster and lowing cows behind (and the rats! don't forget them! Ha!), I tried to tell him again that it might not be too late for Henry and Shannon, that it still might be possible to save them. I heard myself saying *these are things that may be*, as if I were the Spirit of Christmas Yet to Come in the Dickens story. Then I passed out. When I woke up, it was the second of December, and the Western newspapers were reporting 'SWEETHEART BANDITS' ELUDE ELKO POLICE, ESCAPE AGAIN. They hadn't, but no one knew that yet. Except Arlette, of course. And me.

The doctor thought the gangrene hadn't advanced up my forearm, and gambled my life by amputating only my left hand. That was a gamble he won. Five days after being carried into Hemingford City's Angels of Mercy Hospital by Sheriff Jones, I lay wan and ghostly in a hospital bed, 25 pounds lighter and minus my left hand, but alive.

Jones came to see me, his face grave. I waited for him to tell me he was arresting me for the murder of my wife, and then handcuff my remaining hand to the hospital bedpost. But that never happened. Instead, he told me how sorry he was for my loss. My loss! What did that idiot know about loss?

Why am I sitting in this mean hotel room (but not alone!) instead of lying in a murderer's grave? I'll tell you in two words: my mother.

Like Sheriff Jones, she had a habit of peppering her conversation with rhetorical questions. With him it was a conversational device he'd picked up during a lifetime in law enforcement – he asked his silly little questions, then observed the person he was talking to for any guilty reaction: a wince, a frown, a small shift of the eyes. With my mother, it was only a habit of speech she had picked up from her own mother, who was English, and passed on to me. I've lost any faint British accent I might once have had, but never lost my mother's way of turning statements into questions. *You'd better come in now, hadn't you?* she'd say. Or *Your father forgot his lunch again; you'll have to take it to him, won't you?* Even observations about the weather came couched as questions: *Another rainy day, isn't it?*

Although I was feverish and very ill when Sheriff Jones came to the door on that late November day, I wasn't delirious. I remember our conversation clearly, the way a man or woman may remember images from a particularly vivid nightmare.

You need to be grateful to Arlette, because I never would have come out here if not for her, he said.

Dead, I replied.

Sheriff Jones: *She's dead, all right.*

And then, speaking as I had learned to speak at my mother's knee: *I killed her, didn't I?*

Sheriff Jones took my mother's rhetorical device (and his own, don't forget) as a real question. Years later – it was in the factory where I found work after I lost the farm – I heard a foreman berating a clerk for sending an order

to Des Moines instead of Davenport before the clerk had
gotten the shipping form from the front office. *But we
always send the Wednesday orders to Des Moines*, the soon-to-
be-fired clerk protested. *I simply assumed—*

Assume makes an ass out of you and *me*, the foreman
replied. An old saying, I suppose, but that was the first time
I heard it. And is it any wonder that I thought of Sheriff
Frank Jones when I did? My mother's habit of turning
statements into questions saved me from the electric chair.
I was never tried by a jury for the murder of my wife.

Until now, that is.

They're here with me, a lot more than twelve, lined up
along the baseboard all the way around the room, watching
me with their oily eyes. If a maid came in with fresh
sheets and saw those furry jurors, she would run, shrieking,
but no maid will come; I hung the DO NOT DISTURB
sign on the door two days ago, and it's been there ever
since. I haven't been out. I could order food sent up from
the restaurant down the street, I suppose, but I suspect
food would set them off. I'm not hungry, anyway, so it's
no great sacrifice. They have been patient so far, my jurors,
but I suspect they won't be for much longer. Like any
jury, they're anxious for the testimony to be done so they
can render a verdict, receive their token fee (in this case
to be paid in flesh), and go home to their families. So I
must finish. It won't take long. The hard work is done.

What Sheriff Jones said when he sat down beside my hospital
bed was, 'You saw it in my eyes, I guess. Isn't that right?'

I was still a very sick man, but enough recovered to
be cautious. 'Saw what, Sheriff?'

'What I'd come to tell you. You don't remember, do
you? Well, I'm not surprised. You were one sick American,
Wilf. I was pretty sure you were going to die, and I thought

you might do it before I got you back to town. I guess God's not done with you yet, is he?'

Something wasn't done with me, but I doubted if it was God.

'Was it Henry? Did you come out to tell me something about Henry?'

'No,' he said, 'it was Arlette I came about. It's bad news, the worst, but you can't blame yourself. It's not like you beat her out of the house with a stick.' He leaned forward. 'You might have got the idea that I don't like you, Wilf, but that's not true. There's some in these parts who don't – and we know who they are, don't we? – but don't put me in with them just because I have to take their interests into account. You've irritated me a time or two, and I believe that you'd still be friends with Harl Cotterie if you'd kept your boy on a tighter rein, but I've always respected you.'

I doubted it, but kept my lip buttoned.

'As for what happened to Arlette, I'll say it again, because it bears repeating: you can't blame yourself.'

I couldn't? I thought *that* was an odd conclusion to draw even for a lawman who would never be confused with Sherlock Holmes.

'Henry's in trouble, if some of the reports I'm getting are true,' he said heavily, 'and he's dragged Shan Cotterie into the hot water with him. They'll likely boil in it. That's enough for you to handle without claiming responsibility for your wife's death, as well. You don't have to—'

'Just tell me,' I said.

Two days previous to his visit – perhaps the day the rat bit me, perhaps not, but around that time – a farmer headed into Lyme Biska with the last of his produce had spied a trio of coydogs fighting over something about twenty yards north of the road. He might have gone on if he hadn't also spied a scuffed ladies' patent leather shoe and a pair of pink step-ins lying in the ditch. He stopped, fired his rifle to scare off the coys, and advanced into the field to inspect their prize. What he found was a woman's skeleton with the rags of a dress and a few bits of flesh still hanging from it. What remained of her hair was a listless brown, the color to which Arlette's rich auburn might have gone after months out in the elements.

'Two of the back teeth were gone,' Jones said. 'Was Arlette missing a couple of back teeth?'

'Yes,' I lied. 'Lost them from a gum infection.'

'When I came out that day just after she ran off, your boy said she took her good jewelry.'

'Yes.' The jewelry that was now in the well.

'When I asked if she could have laid her hands on any money, you mentioned 200 dollars. Isn't that right?'

Ah yes. The fictional money Arlette had supposedly taken from my dresser. 'That's right.'

He was nodding. 'Well, there you go, there you go. Some jewelry and some money. That explains everything, wouldn't you say?'

'I don't see—'

'Because you're not looking at it from a lawman's point of view. She was robbed on the road, that's all. Some bad egg spied a woman hitchhiking between Hemingford and Lyme Biska, picked her up, killed her, robbed her of her money and her jewelry, then carried her body far enough into the nearest field so it couldn't be seen from the road.' From his long face I could see he was thinking she had probably been raped as well as robbed, and that it was probably a good thing that there wasn't enough of her left to tell for sure.

'That's probably it, then,' I said, and somehow I was able to keep a straight face until he was gone. Then I turned over, and although I thumped my stump in doing so, I began to laugh. I buried my face in my pillow, but not even that would stifle the sound. When the nurse – an ugly old battle-axe – came in and saw the tears streaking my face, she assumed (which makes an ass out of you *and* me) that I had been crying. She softened, a thing I would have thought impossible, and gave me an extra morphine pill. I was, after all, the grieving husband and bereft father. I deserved comfort.

And do you know why I was laughing? Was it Jones's well-meaning stupidity? The fortuitous appearance of a dead female hobo who might have been killed by her male traveling companion while they were drunk? It was both of those things, but mostly it was the shoe. The farmer had only stopped to investigate what the coydogs were fighting over because he'd seen a ladies' patent leather shoe in the ditch. But when Sheriff Jones had asked about footwear that day at the house the previous summer, I'd told him Arlette's *canvas* shoes were the ones that were gone. The idiot had forgotten.

And he never remembered.

When I got back to the farm, almost all my livestock was dead. The only survivor was Achelois, who looked at me with reproachful, starveling eyes and lowed plaintively. I fed her as lovingly as you might feed a pet, and really, that was all she was. What else would you call an animal that can no longer contribute to a family's livelihood?

There was a time when Harlan, assisted by his wife, would have taken care of my place while I was in the hospital; it's how we neighbored out in the middle. But even after the mournful blat of my dying cows started drifting across the fields to him while he sat down to his supper, he stayed away. If I'd been in his place, I might have done the same. In Harl Cotterie's view (and the world's), my son hadn't been content just to ruin his daughter; he'd followed her to what should have been a place of refuge, stolen her away, and forced her into a life of crime. How that 'Sweetheart Bandits' stuff must have eaten into her father! Like acid! Ha!

The following week – around the time the Christmas decorations were going up in farmhouses and along Main Street in Hemingford Home – Sheriff Jones came out to the farm again. One look at his face told me what his news was, and I began to shake my head. 'No. No more. I won't have it. I can't have it. Go away.'

I went back in the house and tried to bar the door against him, but I was both weak and one-handed, and he forced his way in easily enough. 'Take hold, Wilf,' he said. 'You'll get through this.' As if he knew what he was talking about.

He looked in the cabinet with the decorative ceramic beer stein on top of it, found my sadly depleted bottle of whiskey, poured the last finger into the stein, and handed it to me. 'Doctor wouldn't approve,' he said, 'but he's not here and you're going to need it.'

The Sweetheart Bandits had been discovered in their final hideout, Shannon dead of the counterman's bullet, Henry of one he had put into his own brain. The bodies had been taken to the Elko mortuary, pending instructions. Harlan Cotterie would see to his daughter, but would have nothing to do with my son. Of course not. I did that myself. Henry arrived in Hemingford by train on the eighteenth of December, and I was at the depot, along with a black funeral hack from Castings Brothers. My picture was taken repeatedly. I was asked questions which I didn't even try to answer. The headlines in both the *World-Herald* and the much humbler *Hemingford Weekly* featured the phrase GRIEVING FATHER.

If the reporters had seen me at the funeral home, however, when the cheap pine box was opened, they would have seen real grief; they could have featured the

phrase SCREAMING FATHER. The bullet my son fired
into his temple as he sat with Shannon's head on his lap
had mushroomed as it crossed his brain and taken out a
large chunk of his skull on the left side. But that wasn't
the worst. His eyes were gone. His lower lip was chewed
away so that his teeth jutted in a grim grin. All that
remained of his nose was a red stub. Before some cop or
sheriff's deputy had discovered the bodies, the rats had
made a merry meal of my son and his dear love.

'Fix him up,' I told Herbert Castings when I could
talk rationally again.

'Mr James . . . sir . . . the damage is . . .'

'I see what the damage is. Fix him up. And get him
out of that shitting box. Put him in the finest coffin you
have. I don't care what it costs. I have money.' I bent and
kissed his torn cheek. No father should have to kiss his
son for the last time, but if any father ever deserved such
a fate, it was I.

Shannon and Henry were both buried out of the
Hemingford Glory of God Methodist Church, Shannon on
the twenty-second and Henry on Christmas Eve. The church
was full for Shannon, and the weeping was almost loud
enough to raise the roof. I know, because I was there, at
least for a little while. I stood in the back, unnoticed, then
slunk out halfway through Reverend Thursby's eulogy. Rev.
Thursby also presided at Henry's funeral, but I hardly need
tell you that the attendance was much smaller. Thursby saw
only one, but there was another. Arlette was there, too, sitting
next to me, unseen and smiling. Whispering in my ear.

*Do you like how things have turned out, Wilf? Was it
worth it?*

Adding in the funeral cost, the burial expenses, the
mortuary expenses, and the cost of shipping the body
home, the disposal of my son's earthly remains cost just
over 300 dollars. I paid out of the mortgage money. What

else did I have? When the funeral was finished, I went home to an empty house. But first I bought a fresh bottle of whiskey.

1922 had one more trick left in its bag. The day after Christmas, a huge blizzard roared out of the Rockies, socking us with a foot of snow and gale-force winds. As dark came down, the snow turned first to sleet and then to driving rain. Around midnight, as I sat in the darkened parlor, doctoring my bellowing stump with little sips of whiskey, a grinding, rending sound came from the back of the house. It was the roof coming down on that side – the part I'd taken out the mortgage, at least in part, to fix. I toasted it with my glass, then had another sip. When the cold wind began to blow in around my shoulders, I took my coat from its hook in the mudroom, put it on, then sat back down and drank a little more whiskey. At some point I dozed. Another of those grinding crashes woke me around three o'clock. This time it was the front half of the barn that had collapsed. Achelois survived yet again, and the next night I took her into the house with me. Why? you might ask me, and my answer would be, Why not? Just why the hell not? We were the survivors. We were the survivors.

On Christmas morning (which I spent sipping whiskey in my cold sitting room, with my surviving cow for company), I counted what was left of the mortgage money, and realized it would not begin to cover the damage done by the storm. I didn't much care, because I had lost my taste for the farming life, but the thought of the Farrington Company putting up a hog-butchery and polluting the stream still made me grind my teeth in rage. Especially after the high cost I had paid for keeping those triple-goddamned 100 acres out of the company's hands.

It suddenly struck home to me that, with Arlette officially dead instead of missing, those acres were mine. So two days later I swallowed my pride and went to see Harlan Cotterie.

The man who answered my knock had fared better than I, but that year's shocks had taken their toll, just the same. He had lost weight, he had lost hair, and his shirt was wrinkled – although not as wrinkled as his face, and the shirt, at least, would iron out. He looked sixty-five instead of forty-five.

'Don't hit me,' I said when I saw him ball his fists. 'Hear me out.'

'I wouldn't hit a man with only one hand,' he said, 'but I'll thank you to keep it short. And we'll have to talk out here on the stoop, because you are never going to set foot inside my house again.'

'That's fine,' I said. I had lost weight myself – plenty – and I was shivering, but the cold air felt good on my stump, and on the invisible hand that still seemed to exist below it. 'I want to sell you 100 acres of good land, Harl. The hundred Arlette was so determined to sell to the Farrington Company.'

He smiled at that, and his eyes sparkled in their new deep hollows. 'Fallen on hard times, haven't you? Half your house and half your barn caved in. Hermie Gordon says you've got a cow living in there with you.' Hermie Gordon was the rural route mailman, and a notorious gossip.

I named a price so low that Harl's mouth fell open and his eyebrows shot up. It was then that I noticed a smell wafting out of the neat and well-appointed Cotterie farmhouse that seemed entirely alien to that place: burned fried food. Sallie Cotterie was apparently not doing the cooking. Once I might have been interested in such a thing, but that time had passed. All I cared about right then was getting shed of the 100 acres.

It only seemed right to sell them cheap, since they had cost me so dear.

'That's pennies on the dollar,' he said. Then, with evident satisfaction: 'Arlette would roll in her grave.'

She's done more than just roll in it, I thought.

'What are you smiling about, Wilf?'

'Nothing. Except for one thing, I don't care about that land anymore. The one thing I *do* care about is keeping that God damned Farrington slaughter-mill off it.'

'Even if you lose your own place?' He nodded as if I'd asked a question. 'I know about the mortgage you took out. No secrets in a small town.'

'Even if I do,' I agreed. 'Take the offer, Harl. You'd be crazy not to. That stream they'll be filling up with blood and hair and hog intestines – that's your stream, too.'

'No,' he said.

I stared at him, too surprised to say anything. But again he nodded as if I'd asked a question.

'You think you know what you've done to me, but you don't know all of it. Sallie's left me. She's gone to stay with her folks down McCook. She says she may be back, says she'll think things over, but I don't think she will be. So that puts you and me in the same old broke wagon, doesn't it? We're two men who started the year with wives and are ending it without them. We're two men who started the year with living children and are ending it with dead ones. The only difference I can see is that I didn't lose half my house and most of my barn in a storm.' He thought about it. 'And I've still got both hands. There's that, I suppose. When it comes to pulling my peter – should I ever feel the urge to – I'd have a choice of which one to use.'

'What . . . why would she—'

'Oh, use your head. She blames me as well as you

for Shannon's death. She said that if I hadn't gotten on my high horse and sent Shan away, she'd still be alive and living with Henry at your farm just down the road instead of lying frozen in a box underground. She says she'd have a grandchild. She called me a self-righteous fool, and she's right.'

I reached for him with my remaining hand. He slapped it away.

'Don't touch me, Wilf. A single warning on that is all you get.'

I put my hand back at my side.

'One thing I know for sure,' he said. 'If I took you up on that offer, tasty as it is, I'd regret it. Because that land is cursed. We may not agree on everything, but I bet we would on that. If you want to sell it, sell it to the bank. You'll get your mortgage paper back, and some cash besides.'

'They'd just turn around and sell it to Farrington!'

'Tough titty said the kitty' was his final word on it as he closed the door in my face.

On the last day of the year, I drove to Hemingford Home and saw Mr Stoppenhauser at the bank. I told him that I'd decided I could no longer live on the farm. I told him I would like to sell Arlette's acreage to the bank and use the balance of the proceeds to retire the mortgage. Like Harlan Cotterie, he said no. For a moment or two I just sat in the chair facing his desk, not able to believe what I had heard.

'Why not? That's good land!'

He told me that he worked for a bank, and a bank was not a real estate agency. He addressed me as Mr James. My days of being Wilf in that office were over.

'That's just . . .' *Ridiculous* was the word that came to mind, but I didn't want to risk offending him if there was even a chance he might change his mind. Once I had made the decision to sell the land (and the cow, I would have to find a buyer for Achelois, too, possibly a stranger with a bag of magic beans to trade), the idea had taken hold of me with the force of an obsession. So I kept my voice low and spoke calmly.

'That's not exactly true, Mr Stoppenhauser. The bank bought the Rideout place last summer when it came up for auction. The Triple M, as well.'

'Those were different situations. We hold a mortgage on your original 80, and we're content with that. What you do with that hundred acres of pasturage is of no interest to us.'

'Who's been in to see you?' I asked, then realized I didn't have to. 'It was Lester, wasn't it? Cole Farrington's dogsbody.'

'I have no idea what you're talking about,' Stoppenhauser said, but I saw the flicker in his eyes. 'I think your grief and your . . . your injury . . . have temporarily damaged your ability to think clearly.'

'Oh no,' I said, and began to laugh. It was a dangerously unbalanced sound, even to my own ears, 'I've never thought more clearly in my life, sir. He came to see you – him or another, I'm sure Cole Farrington can afford to retain all the shysters he wants – and you made a deal. You *c-c-colluded*!' I was laughing harder than ever.

'Mr James, I'm afraid I'll have to ask you to leave.'

'Maybe you had it all planned out beforehand,' I said. 'Maybe that's why you were so anxious to talk me into the God damned mortgage in the first place. Or maybe when Lester heard about my son, he saw a golden opportunity to take advantage of my misfortune and came running to you. Maybe he sat right in this chair and said, "This is going to work out for both of us, Stoppie – you get the farm, my client gets the land by the crick, and Wilf James can go to Hell." Isn't that pretty much how it went?'

He had pushed a button on his desk, and now the
door opened. It was just a little bank, too small to employ
a security guard, but the teller who leaned in was a beefy
lad. One of the Rohrbacher family, from the look of him;
I'd gone to school with his father, and Henry would have
gone with his younger sister, Mandy.

'Is there a problem, Mr Stoppenhauser?' he asked.

'Not if Mr James leaves now,' he said. 'Won't you see
him out, Kevin?'

Kevin came in, and when I was slow to rise, he clamped
a hand just above my left elbow. He was dressed like a
banker, right down to the suspenders and the bow tie, but
it was a farmer's hand, hard and callused. My still-healing
stump gave a warning throb.

'Come along, sir,' he said.

'Don't pull me,' I said. 'It hurts where my hand used
to be.'

'Then come along.'

'I went to school with your father. He sat beside me
and used to cheat off my paper during Spring Testing
Week.'

He pulled me out of the chair where I had once
been addressed as Wilf. Good old Wilf, who would be a
fool not to take out a mortgage. The chair almost fell
over.

'Happy New Year, Mr James,' Stoppenhauser said.

'And to you, you cozening fuck,' I replied. Seeing
the shocked expression on his face may have been the
last good thing to happen to me in my life. I have sat
here for five minutes, chewing on the end of my pen and
trying to think of one since – a good book, a good meal,
a pleasant afternoon in the park – and I can't.

Kevin Rohrbacher accompanied me across the lobby. I
suppose that is the correct verb; it wasn't quite dragging.

The floor was marble, and our footfalls echoed. The walls were dark oak. At the high tellers' windows, two women served a little group of year-end customers. One of the tellers was young and one was old, but their big-eyed expressions were identical. Yet it wasn't their horrified, almost prurient interest that took my own eye; it was captivated by something else entirely. A burled oak rail three inches wide ran above the tellers' windows, and scurrying busily along it—

'Ware that rat!' I cried, and pointed.

The young teller voiced a little scream, looked up, then exchanged a glance with her older counterpart. There was no rat, only the passing shadow of the ceiling fan. And now everyone was looking at me.

'Stare all you want!' I told them. 'Look your fill! Look until your God damned eyes fall out!'

Then I was in the street, and puffing out cold winter air that looked like cigarette smoke. 'Don't come back unless you have business to do,' Kevin said. 'And unless you can keep a civil tongue.'

'Your father was the biggest God damned cheater I ever went to school with,' I told him. I wanted him to hit me, but he only went back inside and left me alone on the sidewalk, standing in front of my saggy old truck. And that was how Wilfred Leland James spent his visit to town on the last day of 1922.

When I got home, Achelois was no longer in the house. She was in the yard, lying on her side and puffing her own clouds of white vapor. I could see the snow-scuffs where she'd gone galloping off the porch, and the bigger one where she had landed badly and broken both front legs. Not even a blameless cow could survive around me, it seemed.

I went into the mudroom to get my gun, then into the house, wanting to see – if I could – what had frightened her so badly that she'd left her new shelter at a full gallop. It was rats, of course. Three of them sitting on Arlette's treasured sideboard, looking at me with their black and solemn eyes.

'Go back and tell her to leave me alone,' I told them. 'Tell her she's done damage enough. For God's sake tell her to let me be.'

They only sat looking at me with their tails curled around their plump black-gray bodies. So I lifted my varmint rifle and shot the one in the middle. The bullet tore it apart and splattered its leavings all over the wallpaper Arlette had picked out with such care 9 or 10 years before. When Henry was still just a little 'un and things among the three of us were fine.

The other two fled. Back to their secret way underground, I have no doubt. Back to their rotting queen. What they left behind on my dead wife's sideboard were little piles of rat-shit and three or four bits of the burlap sack Henry fetched from the barn on that early summer night in 1922. The rats had come to kill my last cow and bring me little pieces of Arlette's *snood*.

I went outside and patted Achelois on the head. She stretched her neck up and lowed plaintively. *Make it stop. You're the master, you're the god of my world, so make it stop.*

I did.

Happy New Year.

That was the end of 1922, and that is the end of my story; all the rest is epilogue. The emissaries crowded around this room – how the manager of this fine old hotel would scream if he saw them! – will not have to wait much longer to render their verdict. She is the judge, they are the jury, but I'll be my own executioner.

I lost the farm, of course. Nobody, including the Farrington Company, would buy those 100 acres until the home place was gone, and when the hog-butchers finally swooped in, I was forced to sell at an insanely low price. Lester's plan worked perfectly. I'm sure it was his, and I'm sure he got a bonus.

Oh, well; I would have lost my little toehold in Hemingford County even if I'd had financial resources to fall back on, and there is a perverse sort of comfort in that. They say this depression we are in started on Black Friday of last year, but people in states like Kansas, Iowa, and Nebraska, know it started in 1923, when the crops that survived the terrible storms that spring were killed in the drought that followed, a drought that lasted for 2 years. The few crops that did find their way to the big city markets and the small city agricultural exchanges brought a beggar's price. Harlan Cotterie hung on until 1925 or so, and then the bank took his farm. I happened on that news while perusing the Bank Sales items in the *World-Herald*. By 1925, such items sometimes took up whole pages in the newspaper. The small farms had begun to go, and I believe that in a hundred years – maybe only 75 – they'll all be gone. Come 2030 (if there is such a year), all Nebraska west of Omaha will be one big farm. Probably it will be owned by the Farrington Company, and those unfortunate enough to live on that land will pass their existence under dirty yellow skies and wear gas masks to keep from choking on the stench of dead hogs. And *every* stream will run red with the blood of slaughter.

Come 2030, only the rats will be happy.

That's pennies on the dollar, Harlan said on the day I offered to sell him Arlette's land, and eventually I was forced to sell to Cole Farrington for even fewer on the dollar. Andrew Lester, attorney-at-law, brought the papers to the Hemingford City rooming house where I was then living, and he smiled as I signed them. Of course he did. The big boys always win. I was a fool to think it could ever be any different. I was a fool, and everyone I ever loved paid the price. I sometimes wonder if Sallie Cotterie ever came back to Harlan, or if he went to her in McCook after he lost the farm. I don't know, but I think Shannon's death probably ended that previously happy marriage. Poison spreads like ink in water.

Meanwhile, the rats have begun to move in from the baseboards of this room. What was a square has become a closing circle. They know that this is just the *after*, and nothing that comes after an irrevocable act matters much. Yet I will finish. And they won't have me while I'm alive; the final small victory will be mine. My old brown jacket is hung on the back of the chair I'm sitting in. The pistol is in the pocket. When I've finished the last few pages of this confession, I'll use it. They say suicides and murderers go to Hell. If so, I will know my way around, because I've been there for the last eight years.

I went to Omaha, and if it is indeed a city of fools, as I used to claim, then I was at first a model citizen. I set to work drinking up Arlette's 100 acres, and even at pennies on the dollar, it took 2 years. When I wasn't drinking, I visited the places Henry had been during the last months of his life: the grocery and gasoline station in Lyme Biska with the Blue Bonnet Girl on the roof (by then closed with a sign on the boarded-up door reading FOR SALE BY BANK), the pawnshop on Dodge Street (where I emulated my son and bought the pistol now in my jacket pocket), the Omaha branch of the First Agricultural. The pretty young teller still worked there, although her last name was no longer Penmark.

'When I passed him the money, he said thank you,' she told me. 'Maybe he went wrong, but somebody raised him right. Did you know him?'

'No,' I said, 'but I knew his family.'

Of course I went to St Eusebia's, but made no attempt to go in and inquire about Shannon Cotterie to the governess or matron or whatever her title may have been. It was a cold and forbidding hulk of a building, its thick stone and slit windows expressing perfectly how the papist hierarchy seems to feel in their hearts about women. Watching the few pregnant girls who slunk out with downcast eyes and hunched shoulders told me everything I needed to know about why Shan had been so willing to leave it.

Oddly enough, I felt closest to my son in an alley. It was the one next to the Gallatin Street Drug Store & Soda Fountain (Schrafft's Candy & Best Homemade Fudge Our Specialty), two blocks from St Eusebia's. There was a crate there, probably too new to be the one Henry sat on while waiting for a girl adventurous enough to trade information for cigarettes, but I could pretend, and I did. Such pretense was easier when I was drunk, and most days when I turned up on Gallatin Street, I was very drunk indeed. Sometimes I pretended it was 1922 again and it was I who was waiting for Victoria Stevenson. If she came, I would trade her a whole carton of cigarettes to take one message: *When a young man who calls himself Hank turns up here, asking about Shan Cotterie, tell him to get lost. To take his jazz elsewhere. Tell him his father needs him back on the farm, that maybe with two of them working together, they can save it.*

But that girl was beyond my reach. The only Victoria I met was the later version, the one with the three comely children and the respectable title of Mrs Hallett. I had stopped drinking by then, I had a job at the Bilt-Rite Clothing factory, and had reacquainted myself with razor blade and shaving soap. Given this veneer of respectability, she received me willingly enough. I told her who I was only because – if I am to be honest to the end – lying was not an option. I could see in the slight widening of her eyes that she had noted the resemblance.

'Gee, but he was sweet,' she said. 'And so crazy in love. I'm sorry for Shan, too. She was a great gal. It's like a tragedy out of Shakespeare, isn't it?'

Only she said it *trad-a-gee*, and after that I didn't go back to the Gallatin Street alley anymore, because for me Arlette's murder had poisoned even this blameless young Omaha matron's attempt at kindness. She thought Henry and Shannon's deaths were like a trad-a-gee out of Shakespeare. She thought it was romantic. Would she still have thought so, I wonder, if she had heard my wife screaming her last from inside a blood-sodden burlap sack? Or glimpsed my son's eyeless, lipless face?

I held two jobs during my years in the Gateway City, also known as the City of Fools. You will say of *course* I held jobs; I would have been living on the street otherwise. But men more honest than I have continued drinking even when they want to stop, and men more decent than I have ended up sleeping in doorways. I suppose I could say that after my lost years, I made one more effort to live an actual life. There were times when I actually believed that, but lying in bed at night (and listening to the rats scampering in the walls – they have been my constant companions), I always knew the truth: I was still trying to win. Even after Henry and Shannon's deaths, even after losing the farm, I was trying to beat the corpse in the well. She and her *minions*.

John Hanrahan was the storage foreman at the Bilt-Rite factory. He didn't want to hire a man with only one hand, but I begged for a trial, and when I proved to him that I could pull a pallet fully loaded with shirts or overalls as well as any man on his payroll, he took me on. I hauled those pallets for 14 months, and often limped back to the boardinghouse where I was staying with my back and stump on fire. But I never complained, and I even found time to learn sewing. This I did on my lunch hour (which was actually 15 minutes long), and during my afternoon break. While the other men were out back on the loading dock, smoking and telling dirty jokes, I was teaching myself to sew seams, first in the burlap shipping bags we used, and then in the overalls that were the company's main stock-in-trade. I turned out to have a knack for it; I could even lay in a zipper, which is no mean skill on a garment assembly line. I'd press my stump on the garment to hold it in place as my foot ran the electric treadle.

Sewing paid better than hauling, and it was easier on my back, but the Sewing Floor was dark and cavernous, and after four months or so I began to see rats on the mountains of freshly blued denim and hunkering in the shadows beneath the hand-trucks that first brought in the piecework and then rolled it out again.

On several occasions I called the attention of my co-workers to these vermin. They claimed not to see them. Perhaps they really did not. I think it far more likely that they were afraid the Sewing Floor might be temporarily closed down so the ratcatchers could come in and do their work. The sewing crew might have lost three days' wages, or even a week. For men and women with families, that would have been catastrophic. It was easier for them to tell Mr Hanrahan that I was seeing things. I understood. And when they began to call me Crazy Wilf? I understood that, too. It wasn't why I quit.

I quit because the rats kept moving in.

I had been putting a little money away, and was prepared to live on it while I looked for another job, but I didn't have to. Only three days after leaving Bilt-Rite, I saw an

ad in the paper for a librarian at the Omaha Public Library
– must have references or a degree. I had no degree, but
I have been a reader my whole life, and if the events of
1922 taught me anything, it was how to deceive. I forged
references from public libraries in Kansas City and
Springfield, Missouri, and got the job. I felt sure Mr
Quarles would check the references and discover they
were false, so I worked at becoming the best librarian in
America, and I worked fast. When my new boss confronted
me with my deception, I would simply throw myself on
his mercy and hope for the best. But there was no confron-
tation. I held my job at the Omaha Public Library for
four years. Technically speaking, I suppose I still hold it
now, although I haven't been there in a week and have
not phoned in sick.

The rats, you see. They found me there, too. I began
to see them crouched on piles of old books in the
Binding Room, or scuttering along the highest shelves
in the stacks, peering down at me knowingly. Last week,
in the Reference Room, I pulled out a volume of the
Encyclopaedia Britannica for an elderly patron (it was
Ra-St, which no doubt contains an entry for *Rattus
norvegicus*, not to mention *slaughterhouse*) and saw a
hungry gray-black face staring out at me from the vacant
slot. It was the rat that bit off poor Achelois's teat. I
don't know how that could be – I'm sure I killed it
– but there was no doubt. I recognized it. How could
I not? There was a scrap of burlap, *bloodstained* burlap,
caught in its whiskers.

Snood!

I brought the volume of *Britannica* to the old lady
who had requested it (she wore an ermine stole, and the
thing's little black eyes regarded me bleakly). Then I simply
walked out. I wandered the streets for hours, and eventually came here, to the Magnolia Hotel. And here I have

been ever since, spending the money I have saved as a librarian – which doesn't matter any longer – and writing my confession, which does. I—

One of them just nipped me on the ankle. As if to say *Get on with it, time's almost up.* A little blood has begun to stain my sock. It doesn't disturb me, not in the slightest. I have seen more blood in my time; in 1922 there was a room filled with it.

And now I think I hear . . . is it my imagination? No.

Someone has come visiting.

I plugged the pipe, but the rats still escaped. I filled in the well, but *she* also found her way out. And this time I don't think she's alone. I think I hear two sets of shuffling feet, not just one. Or—

Three? Is it three? Is the girl who would have been my daughter-in-law in a better world with them as well?

I think she is. Three corpses shuffling up the hall, their faces (what remains of them) disfigured by rat-bites, Arlette's cocked to one side as well . . . by the kick of a dying cow.

Another bite on the ankle.

And another!

How the management would—

Ow! Another. But they won't have me. And my visitors won't, either, although now I can see the doorknob turning and I can smell them, the remaining flesh hanging on their bones giving off the stench of slaughtered

slaught

The gun

god where is the

stop

OH MAKE THEM STOP BITING M

* * *

From the Omaha *World-Herald*, April 14, 1930

LIBRARIAN COMMITS SUICIDE IN
LOCAL HOTEL
Bizarre Scene Greets Hotel Security Man

The body of Wilfred James, a librarian at the Omaha Public Library, was found in a local hotel on Sunday when efforts by hotel staff to contact him met with no response. The resident of a nearby room had complained of 'a smell like bad meat,' and a hotel chambermaid reported hearing 'muffled shouting or crying, like a man in pain' late Friday afternoon.

After knocking repeatedly and receiving no response, the hotel's Chief of Security used his pass-key and discovered the body of Mr James, slumped over the room's writing desk. 'I saw a pistol and assumed he had shot himself,' the security man said, 'but no one had reported a gunshot, and there was no smell of expended powder. When I checked the gun, I determined it was a badly maintained .25, and not loaded.

'By then, of course, I had seen the blood. I have never seen anything like that before, and never want to again. He had bitten himself all over – arms, legs, ankles, even his toes. Nor was that all. It was clear he had been busy with some sort of writing project, but he had chewed up the paper, as well. It was all over the floor. It looked like paper does when rats chew it up to make their nests. In the end, he chewed his own wrists open. I believe that's what killed him. He certainly must have been deranged.'

Little is known of Mr James at this writing. Ronald Quarles, the head librarian at the Omaha Public Library, took Mr James on in late 1926. 'He was obviously down on his luck, and handicapped by the loss of a hand, but he knew his books and his references were good,' Quarles said. 'He was collegial but distant. I believe he had been doing factory work before applying for a position here, and he told people that before losing his hand, he had owned a small farm in Hemingford County.'

The *World-Herald* is interested in the unfortunate Mr James, and solicits information from any readers who may have known him. The body is being held at the Omaha County Morgue, pending disposition by next of kin. 'If no next of kin appears,' said Dr Tattersall, the Morgue's Chief Medical Officer, 'I suppose he will be buried in public ground.'

AUTHOR'S NOTE

1922 was inspired by a nonfiction book called *Wisconsin Death Trip* (1973), written by Michael Lesy and featuring photographs taken in the small city of Black River Falls, Wisconsin. I was impressed by the rural isolation of these photographs and the harshness and deprivation in the faces of many of the subjects. I wanted to get that feeling in my story.

STEPHEN KING

APT PUPIL

*You must realize that your fate
and my own are now inextricably entwined.*

Todd Bowden is an apt pupil. Good grades, good
family, a paper route. But he is about to meet a
different kind of teacher, Mr Dussander, and to learn
all about Dussander's dark and deadly past . . . a
decades-old manhunt Dussander has escaped to this day.

Yet Todd doesn't want to turn his teacher in. Todd
wants to know more. Much more. He is about to
face his fears and learn the real meaning of power –
and the seductive lure of evil.

A classic story from Stephen King – adapted into a
movie starring Ian McKellen – *Apt Pupil* reveals layers
upon layers of deception and horror as the boy and
old man hold each other in a mutual deathgrip.
Each knows something the other wants kept secret.

**'Not since Dickens has a writer had so
many readers by the throat'** *GUARDIAN*

HODDER

STEPHEN KING

THE BODY

*We'd all listened to the Ray Brower story . . .
he was a kid our age.*

The small town of Castle Rock is tuning in
to the news of a young boy who has gone
missing from a nearby town.

Gordie Lachance and his three friends set off along
the railway tracks on a quest, determined to become
famous by officially finding the boy's body.

But their journey becomes a rite of passage, and as they
cross the railway trestle and the tracks begin to hum, the
boys encounter an intimation of their own mortality.

An iconic exploration of friendship, loneliness and
adventure adapted into the classic 1986 film *Stand by
Me*, *The Body* is an unforgettable coming-of-age story
by master chronicler of small-town adolescence and
universal experience, Stephen King.

'An incredibly gifted writer' *GUARDIAN*

HODDER

STEPHEN KING

THE LANGOLIERS

The flight attendants were gone; almost all the passengers were gone; Brian Engle was willing to bet the 767's two-man cockpit crew was also gone. He believed Flight 29 was heading east on automatic pilot.

On a red-eye flight from Los Angeles to Boston, ten passengers wake up to discover everyone else has disappeared. Brian Engle, a trained pilot, remembers something about a strange aurora borealis and turbulence reports over the desert. Now he has to try to land the plane.

But the safe haven of Bangor airport is not what it seems. It's eerily empty. The clocks have stopped. The food and drink is tasteless. The fuel won't burn. And the sound, like 'radio static', is getting closer. Craig Toomy, an investment banker, believes he knows what's coming. The Langoliers. Which means time is, quite literally, running out . . .

A spine-tingling, propulsive novella, *The Langoliers* is a brilliant read from the masterful Stephen King.

'*The Langoliers* is . . . harrowing . . . It's a great idea, with the execution both grounded and terrifying' GUARDIAN

HODDER

STEPHEN KING

THE MIST

A man staggered into the market . . .
'Something in the fog!' he screamed.

Following a freak summer storm, David Drayton, his son Billy, and their neighbour Brent Norton join dozens of others and head to the local grocery store to replenish supplies.

Once there, they become trapped by a strange mist that has enveloped the town. Violent forces concealed in the mist are starting to emerge. And there is another shocking threat from within – one group of survivors, led by a religious zealot, is calling for a sacrifice.

Now David and his son must try to escape.
But what's outside may be even more dangerous.

This exhilarating novella which was the basis of a major motion picture by Frank Darabont explores the horror in both the enemy you know – and the one you can only imagine.

'[King's] genius remains in the conjuring of evil out of ephemera, of a malevolent universe lurking behind the Walmart shopping trolley banality of everyday, small-town America' *THE TIMES*

HODDER

STEPHEN KING

RITA HAYWORTH AND
SHAWSHANK
REDEMPTION

*There's a guy like me in every state and federal prison in America,
I guess — I'm the guy who can get it for you.*

And new convict Andy Dufresne wants two things from
fellow prisoner Red: a small rock-hammer for carving stones
and a giant poster of Rita Hayworth.

So begins this mesmerising tale of unjust imprisonment,
deep friendship and offbeat escape.

Rita Hayworth and Shawshank Redemption is one of King's most
celebrated stories, and it helped make Castle Rock a place readers
would return to over and over again. Suspenseful, heart-wrenching
and hopeful, this iconic King novella is populated by a cast of
unforgettable characters, especially the fiercely compelling convict
named Andy Dufresne who is seeking his ultimate revenge.

Originally published in the collection *Different Seasons*, it was made
into the film *The Shawshank Redemption*. Starring Morgan Freeman
and Tim Robbins, this modern classic was nominated for seven
Academy Awards, including Best Picture, is one of the most beloved
films of all time and is IMDb's top-rated movie of all time.

'One of the great storytellers of our time' *GUARDIAN*

HODDER

STEPHEN KING

THE SUN DOG

It's mine – that was what he had thought when his finger had pushed the shutter-button for the first time. Now he found himself wondering if maybe he hadn't gotten that backward.

Kevin Delevan wants only one thing for his fifteenth birthday: a Polaroid Sun 660.

There's something wrong with his gift, though. No matter where Kevin aims the camera, it produces a photograph of an enormous, vicious dog. In each successive picture, the menacing creature draws nearer to the flat surface of the Polaroid film as if it intends to break through.

When old Pop Merrill, Castle Rock's sharpest trader, gets wind of this phenomenon, he devises a way to profit from it. But the Sun Dog, a beast that shouldn't exist at all, turns out to be a very dangerous investment.

'*The Sun Dog* works beautifully as another addition to those metaphorical stories about King's own personal fears' *GUARDIAN*

HODDER

STEPHEN KING
Chilling Classics

STEPHEN KING

ICONIC STORIES

To find out more about Stephen King,
please visit www.stephenkingbooks.co.uk
or www.facebook.com/stephenkingbooks

HODDER